A Bark in the Night

The Talking Dog Detective Agency
Book One

M K Scott

The Talking Dog Detective Agency

M K Scott

Copyright © 2017

Print Edition

All characters in this book are fictional and figments of the author's imagination.

Chapter One

A GROAN ESCAPED the silent watcher as the girl pulled out a bunch of keys to unlock the front door. The dog that had been sitting now silently stood, his ears alert, his head slowly swinging side to side as he emitted a low growl.

"Damn it." He hadn't counted on a dog. Who takes a dog with them to an office building anyhow? He could have knocked down the girl and grabbed the keys, and finally made it into the building. He'd spent the last six months trying to enter the place.

The few remaining offices weren't open to the public. He'd even donned delivery outfits and tried to get buzzed in. All he managed to discover was no one in the building had water delivered or even a pizza. Usually, he received no reply when he buzzed. It could be that the buzzer didn't work. The building itself was circa 1930s and only the bottom floor was stores, while the rest were apartments or offices.

That would have worked fine if there was an actual store on the first floor instead of empty rooms. He'd considered breaking in, but he'd most likely get caught and end up back in the slammer. Something he'd prefer to avoid since he had more enemies inside than he did out. Now, he'd have to rethink the situation. Once the girl and her dog entered the building, he tucked his hands into his jacket pocket to feel the short length of pipe he'd hidden there. A man had to protect himself, but as a felon, a gun would automatically earn a huge fine and possibly incarceration. Things he wanted to avoid.

Hands still in pockets, he strolled in the direction of Monument Circle. Sweat dotted his face due to the early heat wave. He could have pulled off his sweatshirt, but the hoodie provided conformity that made him almost invisible.

In the center of the city stood a huge war monument reaching toward the heavens as if trying to touch the departed or at least send a message they hadn't been forgotten. He couldn't remember when it had been built—sometime after the Civil War. As a kid, his grandfather had taken him there. With each war, more statues and flat memorials engraved with names appeared. He remembered fingering the names thinking the people only became important by dying. That wasn't going to be him. Nope, he'd had enough of being Toby Nobody. Once he got into the building, he'd find what was his by right and buy that sailboat he fantasized about while doing time. Might even sail around the world.

Foot and vehicle traffic picked up as he made his way to the circle. A horse-driven carriage, complete with picture-snapping tourists, passed him on one side. The harness bells jingled with the horse's movements. He was not sure why a person would even bell a horse. The animal was too large to miss. Then again, maybe the owner thought it made the experience more festive. Toby stopped and watched the slow-moving carriage. He'd never taken a carriage ride, never took a gondola ride down the canal, either. Nope, those things were for tourists or people with a lot of throwaway money. Soon, that would be him, as soon as he got rid of the obstacles.

NALA PLACED ONE hand on her hip and kept a tight grip on the leash clipped to a handsome black German shepherd mix as she surveyed the building. The stone façade building rose a good five stories, nothing compared to the other buildings looming behind it on a more visited street in Indianapolis. The morning sun revealed chipped bricks and the crumbling entrance steps, exposing the underlying concrete block structure.

"The building has character." She glanced up and down the street, noticing the lack of foot traffic during the early day. The ground floor windows revealed empty rooms inside where light spots on the industrial gray carpet revealed where furniture once sat. "I was never shown a ground floor office or even one with wraparound windows." Her shoulders went up in a shrug. "It is just as well. Anyone visiting a private eye doesn't want to be on display. I probably couldn't afford it anyhow. Let's go see *our* office."

The dog gave a bark as if he understood. Nala's straight hair swung into her face as she bent to pat the animal. "That's right, Max. It's a new start for both of us."

Max and Nala climbed the first flight of stairs in silence. By the time they reached the second flight, a young man with a dark hipster beard and arms full of labeled boxes met them.

"Hey, a dog, cool!"

A bark greeted his assessment while Nala offered her hand, then pulled it back as she realized he couldn't shake. "Hello. Do you need any help with your boxes?"

"No, I'm good. I'm sure you're not coming to see me. I'd remember if I had a beautiful woman and her equally handsome dog coming to see me."

A nervous laugh greeted his remark. Blatant flirting rattled Nala since it was difficult to pinpoint if it was sincere. Extroverts could reply with clever comebacks in a second, while people like herself struggled for an appropriate reply long after the person had left. "Yeah, right."

Instead of insisting he meant it, the man grinned. "I'm Harry Chafant. I run a mail-order business on the second floor. Didn't know there were any other businesses in the building. There are some apartments in use, though. Maybe you're here to see one of the residents."

Nala shoved her hands in her jeans pockets since she didn't know what to do with them. "Ah, I'm Nala, Nala Bonne." *Oops*, she had lost a chance to try out her new name. "I'll be opening my business on the third floor. Max," she gestured to her dog, "and I are going up to check out the office."

"Really?" Harry drew out the word, and his smile grew bigger. "Today must be my lucky day. I'm headed to the post office, but when I get back, I'd love to show you around."

"Thanks, but I've already seen the building." Regret stabbed her as she watched the man's smile slip. No good would come out of being too friendly to her neighbors. Even if they did hit it off, eventually they'd break up and she'd peer out her door every time a woman got buzzed in, wondering if it was her replacement. Still, she didn't want to sound unfriendly. She held up one hand. "See ya around."

"Yeah," Harry agreed and continued to descend the stairs.

If her best friend, Karly, had witnessed the scene, she'd take Nala to task, telling her she shot down another perfectly good prospect. Maybe she had, but she also avoided a messy emotional entanglement and the possibility of placing another crack in her heart. Some women threw themselves into the dating game with all the intensity of a bullfighter. A failed romance never seemed to get them down. They would just move on to the next guy. The most amazing thing about it was that there was always a next guy. In her experience, most men never passed her father's background investigation test. Oh, the joys of having a father in law enforcement.

On the third-floor landing, Nala withdrew her key to the office and opened the door. The entry office remained dusty and empty. The furniture fairies hadn't appeared overnight, not that she'd expected them to. A few words to her mother would have her scouring the design warehouse for office furniture, but she wouldn't mention it. This was something Nala wanted to accomplish on her own. As the only child of overprotective parents, she seldom felt like she did much on her own. Even with school projects, she had felt they were more a group project.

Her father had built a circuit board that allowed an electrical circuit to run several items at once for the science fair. She, however, had wanted to grow plants and play music to them. When she didn't ace the science fair, her father demanded to know if the fair was fixed. It was obvious the circuit board was the superior project. Her petite teacher went toe to toe with her father and pointed out the circuit board was beyond the ability of a seven-year-old. A third-grader won with an experiment that showed tomato plants grew taller with regular shots of diet cola.

"Let's hit it." Nala dropped the leash and allowed Max to wander at will while she withdrew window cleaner, a rag, and some press-on letters. Her first project would be the exterior door.

"I'm not sure about the clear glass. If a person wants privacy, they don't want everyone and their cousin peering in at them as they come to me to consult about a philandering husband or wife."

"Do people even do that anymore? I just thought they divorced, divvied up the stuff, and sometimes offloaded the family pet to a friend, relative, or took him for a ride in the country."

Nala blinked, knowing good and well no one else was in the office. She dropped her gaze to Max, who had his head cocked as if waiting for her answer. *No, it couldn't be.* Dogs didn't talk, at least not in a raspy baritone. She pinched herself just to be certain she wasn't dreaming. It hurt. *Maybe she just thought he said something. The best thing would be to test out her theory.* "Did your last owners divorce?"

Something must have happened to Max since she had picked him up at an animal shelter the day before he would have been put down. Grown dogs were only kept for a few days at the most. Then again, it could be she wanted Max to talk so she'd have someone to converse with. A fellow traveler in this new life she'd plotted out for herself.

"Nope." He grimaced, showing his teeth. "I made the mistake of talking again. Not the first time I've been ousted from a comfortable home. This last time I was driven from the house by my former owner holding a crucifix and calling me *devil dog.*"

"Weird." She shook her head hard still not convinced she wasn't dreaming. I would have thought someone would have put you on the David Letterman show. Whoops, I keep forgetting he retired." *Was she really having a conversation with her dog?*

"You'd think that." He barked a couple of times before continuing. "You gotta remember English is my third language and some things don't translate."

"You speak three languages?"

He lifted his nose with pride. "I do. Dog, of course, the silent language of scent, and I'm reasonably conversant in English. One potential owner tried to speak to me in German. Despite my muddied bloodlines, I couldn't understand a word he said. I wanted to tell him I was born in America. I didn't, since I wasn't totally sure."

"Ah, of course." She nodded her head as if she understood. *Was there anything understandable about a talking dog?* "So, when did you start talking? Are there a lot of talking dogs out there?"

His nose dropped as he stretched out and laid his head on his paws. "All dogs talk in the accepted canine dialect, except for basenjis who do this strange yodeling thing. I haven't met one who speaks English, although most do understand it very well. They might pretend not to know phrases such as stay off the couch, not for you, or not now. They do. Even though they understand English, they freak out when I say something. Something about it being us against them, meaning your kind."

"Ah." Nala searched her mind for how she had treated Max in the few days she owned him. Had she offended him somehow by treating him like a dog? "You never answered how you came to talk."

"Oh, that." He managed a few sharp yips that resembled a laugh. "Funny story. My first owner was a close-mouthed male. Not one to share his feelings or general observations about life. While this didn't bother me all that much, it was an entirely different story for his girlfriend, who happened to be a witch. She always fixed extra scrambled eggs and bacon for me when she visited, so I liked her. Anyhow, one day, she says to the man, 'If you don't talk to me, then your dog will.'"

"Just like that?"

"Took me a while to become a good conversationalist. At the time, I was so excited I voiced every thought." He lifted his head enough to display a doggy grin. "Imagine a constant litany of me listing everything I saw. Tree, grass, dog poop from the poodle two houses down, smells like she likes me. After all, she left it in front of my house. Well, you get the idea."

"Irritating."

"Yep, I discovered immediately that while people yack non-stop, they don't appreciate a talkative dog, especially my first owner who didn't even make the effort to talk to his girlfriend. One day, she was gone. Not sure if they agreed to separate. I just noticed the house smelled less like the sandalwood incense she always burned. After that, I got relocated, too."

"Where?"

"A family with kids. They had a little boy I adored. He wasn't that good at walking so he often hung onto me when he was unstable. It was only natural that I tried to encourage him. His parents were worried about his developing psyche and the dangers of believing a dog could talk. They thought I was a bad influence." Max stood, paced to the hallway and returned to his original place before circling and flopping back down on the floor.

"That's too bad about the kid. I'm not sure what I'll do with a talking dog."

A foul smell permeated the air. "Sorry." Max offered her an apologetic expression. "The Chinese food you gave me yesterday doesn't agree with me. I love it, though. Besides, stress has that effect, too."

Her intention had been to get a dog for companionship. Karly, who worked at the shelter, had emailed her pictures of dogs that would be put down. *Talk about guilt.* Even worse, when they met for lunch, she'd talk about the abandoned dogs, giving them names and listing their idiosyncrasies. Nala pointed out more than once that if

Karly wanted someone to adopt a dog it was better not to mention things such as its tendency to rip up anything vaguely chewable or its midnight howling. Karly insisted people had to enter relationships with open eyes.

As if that would ever work. There was a reason women shoved themselves into shapewear, piled on the makeup, and clipped on hair extensions. Men didn't want reality, and she was sure women didn't either. On occasion, when they needed a reality check, they'd hire an investigator. She'd specialize in date research. No woman wanted to go on a date with an online prospect or even the cousin of a co-worker and end up battered, broke or, worse, dead.

"We'll have to limit your intake to the weekends. Can't have you scaring off the clients with your toxic farts."

A hopeful gleam appeared in Max's eyes as his ears pitched forward. "Do you mean you're going to keep me?"

"Why not?"

"The talking usually scares people off, but Karly assured me you'd be okay with it. Since you're into magic, psychic skills, and all that." His long tail wagged, hitting the floor. The empty room magnified the sound.

"Karly knew? The woman who never believes in too much information withheld the fact from me that you could speak?"

"She never told you she didn't like Jeff, either."

Nala looked up from pecking at her cell with her index finger. "You mean you and Karly talked about my ex-boyfriend?"

Max swallowed hard. "You know, I could be an immense help around the detective agency."

"How so?"

"Scent. I can tell if people are lying or not by their scent."

She shook her head, imagining how well a large German shepherd mix sniffing them would go over. "I'm pretty sure my future clients and suspects wouldn't go for you sticking your nose in their crotch."

"Please." He managed a huff. "I have excellent scent ability. The nose in the crotch thing is something dogs do just for fun. It's a game we like to play with humans. If you didn't react so strongly, then it wouldn't be as hilarious."

Chapter Two

THE OUTER OFFICE door sparkled after Nala scrubbed it four times, ridding it of decades of grease and grime. If there had been any lettering on it previously, it didn't show. Peel and stick letters would have to do until she got the money to create a name plaque or have her name painted on the door.

She knelt on the floor, spreading out the letters spelling out N JONES, PRIVATE INVESTIGATOR. DISCREET INQUIRIES. Perhaps she shouldn't put the last part up. Her grandfather joked he never trusted anyone who extolled their own product, saying a baker who referred to his cookies as delicious did so because no one else would. As she huddled over the letters, trying to decide if she should forget the last line, the click of dog nails drew nearer.

"What's with N Jones? Is someone else going to be working here?" His ears flicked forward as if waiting for an answer.

How did she rate both a talking and nosy pooch? Her lips twisted as she considered what to say when a thought hit her. "You can read, too?"

Max's mouth dropped open and his long tongue lolled out. He stood staring at Nala before closing his mouth and shaking his head. "How about that? I never tried to read until now, and I can!" He let out a small howl and pranced around in a small circle. "Look at me,

I can read! Didn't even go to school. I got it all over humans who have to struggle to read." His voice took on a delighted quality as he chanted his reading ability over and over.

"Enough!" Nala stood and clapped her hands together twice. "It was a spell. You can only read and talk because of a spell. You never actually learned."

"Sez you. I could have learned. I bet your partner N Jones will be nicer to me."

A small snort escaped her, realizing she'd take Max down a few notches. *Wait, was she fighting with a dog?* "I'm N Jones."

"No, you're Nala Bonne. Karly said your name several times when talking to me."

"Figures."

"So, what's with N Jones? Do you have spelling issues? Maybe I can help. Obviously, I'm a great reader. Makes sense that I'd be a good speller, too. Let me think about this. *Nala*. N.Y.L.A."

She shook her index finger at Max. "You're wrong. It's N A L A. Besides, I want to sound tough since I'm not a preschool teacher anymore. Nala Bonne is a soft and fluffy name, which is great for preschool but not for a PI. I need something that sounds tough."

"Why not Stone or Hammer?"

"That's not a bad idea. I like it. There was a fictional gumshoe named Mike Hammer. The guy was as tough as nails. I could be N Hammer."

"Why not Nala Hammer?"

Her eyes rolled upward. While a dog could talk and read like a human, it couldn't reason like one. "Some people don't want a female P.I."

"Won't they notice you're not a man? It's my experience humans miss a great deal. Still, I think they'd notice."

"Yeah, but by then, the person would be in my office, and I'd win them over with my charm…"

Max managed a cough.

Nala continued undeterred, "…and my wide-open schedule and low prices. All I want to do is get my foot in the door."

"Been there, although it was usually my nose I tried to get in the door. I figured I'd used my liquid brown eyes to seal the deal, and you can see how well that worked out."

"Hey! I picked you."

"No, you didn't. After about a week of Karly calling you endlessly about a dog that would be perfect for you, you showed up right before," he paused to shudder, "*the chamber*. The other dogs had already said their final goodbyes to me."

"Oh, my goodness, you poor dear." She dropped to her knees and hugged Max. The buzzer sounded, cutting the hug short. Nala pushed to her feet while Max complained.

"You almost choked me to death."

Before she could comment, the dog winked one eye. Her thumb hit the intercom button. "What is it?"

"Delivery. Wok-n-Roll Chinese."

Her finger slid from the button, resting on the metal panel that housed the button. Not more than two months ago, her friend, Steph, called from New York City to explain an intruder broke into their building by pretending to be a delivery boy and someone buzzed him in. Right now, two locked doors were between her and whoever was on the front steps.

Might as well send the possible criminal on his way. Her thumb depressed the intercom button. "I didn't order Chinese."

"I meant Jose's House of Tacos. I deliver for a lot of places."

As far as she could tell she was the only person in the building since Harry had just left. There was no way she'd open the door. Max made a low, menacing growl. Too bad it didn't carry three stories down. Nala went to the front window without the blinds. She leaned back against the wall and peeked through the window. *Nothing*. Well, nothing useful. She could see the street traffic and the mailman walking down the street.

Just when she was ready to step away from the window, someone slinked away from the building, male, white, middle-aged, shiny spot on the top of the head. She logged the information mentally as he turned and stared up at the window. She flattened herself against the wall, almost sure he hadn't seen her.

Black hoodie, gray sweat pants and no delivery box in sight. She mentally added the details to her list. Her observation skills came from her father drilling her constantly. Sometimes, he'd stick a photo in front of her for five seconds, turn it over, and make her name what she saw. Her mother used to grumble about the game, but her father insisted people needed to be aware of their surroundings. He usually tacked on that most people were horrible eyewitnesses. They had eyes but did not see.

Her father may have considered she might follow him into law enforcement, but she hadn't. Most high school seniors assumed they were deep thinkers with everything figured out, but they weren't. She should know since she went to college with those fellow seniors. Some flunked out before Christmas break their first year. Thank goodness for them, because she shone in comparison. Sure, she enrolled in psychology because about a third of her friends did. College was all about hanging with your friends, right?

Halfway through college she thought acting might be a good career choice after she received rave reviews from friends and family for her role of Mrs. Soames in *Our Town*. That was her theatrical high. When she tried out as an extra in a low-budget movie shooting in town, the agent described her as not being enough of anything. Not tall enough, not blond enough, not curvy enough, not old enough. The list went on forever with him summing it up with, "No one needs another skinny Latino girl." Never got a chance to tell him that Bonne was a French name.

Max strolled over to her and pushed his wet nose into her hand.

"He's gone," she said.

"Let me see." He walked over to the window and placed his paws on the sill. "Don't see anything, except a pigeon."

Nala glanced at the glass. "It's walking on the ledge. Besides, you don't even know what he looks like."

Max dropped his front paws to the floor. "You're telling me you do?"

"Yes. I got a good look at him. I have excellent observation skills."

"Is that what made you decide to be a private investigator?"

"Good question." She walked back to the letters on the floor and knelt back beside them. "I guess having this great awareness of everything going on around me just made me a little crazy as a preschool teacher. From my place in the center of the room, I could see one boy picking his nose and eating the boogers." She shuddered. "Another kid had a pair of scissors to the hair of a girl who always wore an elaborate hair bow. A third boy dressed in a tiny football jersey had a large puddle growing at his feet, while the fourth one had her head buried in my stomach sobbing about something I couldn't understand. Personally, I think I would have been better off not observing so much."

"That's why you quit?"

Nala rocked back on her heels as her eyes rolled up, trying to find that one incident that served as her breaking point. "Hmm, it was more of a combination of things. I worked hard to instill social skills such as sharing, waiting your turn, and politeness only to send the kids home to parents who cussed each other out. Then there were the parents who were raising divas in training and wanted me to rock their child and sing a special calming song to them. There were other parents who talked to me as if I *were* the preschooler. It came to a head when one boy slashed a deep cut on another boy's head with a metal truck. The slasher's parents insisted their son was provoked. That's when I decided there had to be something better."

"I would have bit the boy."

"The other boy did, but that was after he was hit by the truck."

The buzzer sounded again, freezing Nala in the action of gathering up her letters.

Chapter Three

NALA SCRAMBLED INTO a standing position, clutching a handful of letters, then sidled to the metal intercom as if someone might be listening. The buzzer sounded again, startling her into dropping letters that slowly fluttered to the floor, landing with barely a whisper.

A familiar voice came through the tiny speaker. "It's your mother. I've got move-in supplies and lunch."

Nala pressed down the intercom button to respond, but before she could, Max enthused, "Lunch!" The sound of Max's voice surely reached her mother's ears.

Her mother replied, "Is there a man up there? Buzz me in. I want to meet him."

Nala's hand drifted to the second button, aware she'd be admitting a force of nature named Guinevere Bonne into the building. Saying her mother was driven would be an understatement. Being an only child of two Type A personalities was no picnic. Occasionally, they wanted her to experience their missed opportunities. She always figured the reason she sucked at both violin playing and horseback riding was she never wanted to do either.

For years, her mother has been content running Posh Interiors, which had been a blessing since the business took most of her mother's energy. But something happened this year, something horrible. Her mother hadn't contracted an incurable illness or gone bankrupt. Her father hadn't stepped out on her mother, either. To the outside world, everything looked about the same, but it wasn't. The very stylish and organized Guinevere Bonne decided she wanted to be a grandmother. She informed Nala at a family dinner that her yet-to-be-born children would call her Nana Gwen. When her mother wanted something, she always got it.

Maybe she could convince Max to call her Nana Gwen. She gave her dog a measured look. "It will be your first time to meet my mom. Be on your good behavior."

He gave a sharp bark that sounded slightly affronted. Nala stood near the door and tried to see the office the way her mother might see it. As an older building, it had lofty ceilings and long windows that allowed the sunlight to flood in. That was the plus side.

No way her mother would miss the peeling wallpaper that appeared to be taking the plaster with it. Water spots dotted the ceiling, but probably nothing a can of sealer wouldn't fix. The scarred wooden floor remained intact with no missing boards. One window was bare while the other sported mostly broken aluminum blinds.

An interior door opened into a second room, which would be where she conducted her discreet inquiries. The room could easily be called square in shape, especially if a person used the word *small* in front of *square*. Nala strolled over to the window, sniffing the room for a hint of mildew, but it had more of a dry, stale odor. No telling how long the offices had stood empty.

There was an odd square cut on the floor as if someone had tried to make a secret hiding place. Not so secret now with the floor bare. Curious, she fingered the seam wondering if she'd need a crowbar to pry it up. Better to leave it alone. Once it was up, it probably wouldn't fit back into place.

A cheery voice called out. "Whose gorgeous dog? Is there an equally tall, dark, and handsome owner to go with you? Is my daughter and *your* owner up to some risqué escapades?"

Nala's eyes rolled upward as she pushed up from the floor. "No, Mom. Don't get your hopes up. *Risqué escapades,* what is that anyhow? A questionable ice show?"

Instead of replying, her mother stretched to her full height of five-two, in heels, to see around her.

"There's no one here," Nala assured, aware her mother was looking for the owner of the baritone. "You tell her, Max."

"*Woof. Woof.*" He turned his head in Nala's direction and winked.

Her mother ignored them and continued her search. Her kitten heels echoed in the inner office. On her return to the exterior office, her gaze focused on a closed closet door. "You can't fool your mother. I think it's shameful the way you're making," she had her hand on the closet door and opened it with such vigor the wire hangers inside hit each other, "the poor man hide."

Guinevere stuck her head in the closet, possibly doubting the obvious. "I heard a man's voice."

"That was Max." It would help if the dog would decide to talk right about now. She nudged him with her knee, which only resulted in him moving away from her and standing beside her mother.

"Please, Nala, stop the crazy talk." She shot a manicured hand through her dark, short hair. "This nonsense keeps you single, not your domineering manner."

She almost asked what *domineering manner,* but that would be playing into her mother's hands. "Where's lunch?"

"Oh, that, I left it in the hall. I needed my hands free for the door." Her mother gestured to the doorway.

What she didn't say was that she dropped everything, hoping to catch her with an actual guy. Nala peeked into the hall and discovered a pile of abandoned bags along with a broom. "Oh good, a broom. I need one."

Her mother appeared in the hallway lit only by a single window. "I know lunch is in here somewhere." Max joined her and located the food with no problem. Her mother patted him on the head and removed distinctive red and white bags whose aroma evoked memories of dinners around a red and white checkered tablecloth-covered table complete with a candle stuck in a Chianti bottle.

"Bernardoes." Nala breathed the restaurant name with reverence. "Did you get baked ziti?"

"I wouldn't forget your favorite. Plenty of garlic bread, too. Grab the two pop-up stools. Figured you wouldn't have furniture, yet."

Yet was the operative word since she didn't have any office furniture at all. They balanced on tiny stools while Guinevere withdrew a warm, foil-covered pan that exuded rich tomato and garlic scents. "Here's yours. I have silverware, such as it is." She handed over a plastic fork.

Nala peeled the foil off the pan. "This looks yummy."

Max whimpered, reminding her of his foodless state. Her mother threw a breadstick in his general direction, which he snapped out of the air.

"Look at that. What a great trick."

"You'd be surprised at all the tricks he can do."

Max shook his head *no*. What did he mean no? Was she going to be the only person Max ever talked to, except for Karly?

Karly talked to Max since she talked to all the dogs at the shelter, and they all talked back, in their own way. People referred to her friend as the *dog whisperer*, but it would have been more appropriate to call her *the listener*. When canines showed up at the shelter, she not only knew their life story, she also knew the type of owner they needed. A better title might have been the *dog matchmaker*. Her eyes drifted to Max, who had an avid expression trained on her mother who had broken another breadstick in half. That meant fate had brought her and Max together.

Still, most people would freak out if they had a talking dog, especially one with a smart mouth? A few might be amused, while some opportunistic people might try to make money off Max only to discover that he did not talk on cue, which would probably not end well. The fact he'd had so many homes told the story. Surely, she could be a step up in the owner department. After all, a talking dog couldn't be any more trouble than a regular pooch.

"Nala, are you even listening to me?"

Since her eyes were on Max, she blinked, certain his mouth hadn't moved. How had he managed that? Better yet, had his voice morphed into a woman's? Oh, it was her mother. Her eyes shifted to her parent, who regarded her with a skeptical gaze.

"Sorry, Mother, I missed what you said. Could you repeat that?"

Her mother gave a small, disbelieving snort. "More like you didn't want to acknowledge the truth is more like it."

Sheesh, here she goes again. Nala would have to beg to hear whatever she missed. If she didn't, her mother would act affronted. Guinevere Bonne often dabbled in peoples' emotions the ways others took up watercolors. She would not only have you saying and feeling things she wanted, but half the time you could be acting on ideas that were originally hers. A slow breath escaped Nala as she realized whatever her mother said would be something, she'd be best off not hearing. All the same, she did bring lunch. "Tell me again. I was worried about Karly."

Throwing her friend under the bus as a distracting tactic had worked on previous occasions since her mother regarded Karly as her agreeable daughter.

"What's wrong with Karly?"

Max cocked his head as if asking also.

What could be wrong with her affable sidekick? "Oh, nothing really. I just think she spends too much time around dogs. She even talks to them." She confided the last bit in a whisper, but Max heard and responded.

"What's wrong with that?"

Gwen dropped her breadstick and swiveled her head. "There's that voice again. Where is he? He must be a magician?"

"It's Max." She pointed to the dog gobbling down the dropped bread stick.

"Goodness." Her mother shook her head and speared a meatball. "I've read about women who don't have children before thirty forming odd attachments to pets, but there was no mention of thinking their pet could talk."

"He can!" She pointed to Max who had flopped down on the floor, resting his head on his paws. "Speak!" He blinked his brown eyes at her, then closed them. *Really, he was going to play it that way.*

Her mother reached across the foot of space that separated them and patted her knee. "There, there. I'm sure you're becoming unstable because you haven't been able to satisfy your natural urges for a husband and family."

Max opened one eye and smirked.

"I don't have a natural urge for a husband and family."

Her mother clucked. "Deny if you want. I know you want a

career. I did, too. Fortunately, I was able to run Posh Interiors and be a mother at the same time."

No way would Nala point out that her father and the woman who lived next door, Rhoda, had watched her while Gwen consulted with her various clients. Her father sharpened her observation skills while Rhoda tested them by performing magic tricks and daring Nala to figure them out. Her neighbor claimed she was descended from Romany Gypsies. No one knew if it was true, but Nala had picked up some overheard gypsy curses and used them with success to ward off mean girls at school, which unfortunately had resulted in a parent conference.

"I know." While her mother was good at bending people to her will, she had unwittingly passed on some of her skills to Nala. "You've always been my role model. I'm lucky to have such a strong, independent, and beautiful mother."

Her mother beamed. "It's every parent's dream to be truly appreciated by their child."

Well, she didn't know about it being every mother's dream, but she knew it was her mother's. A knock sounded on the door, startling her. Who could that be? Better yet, how did they get into the building?

Chapter Four

HER MOTHER CALMLY ate her pasta while Nala answered the door. Maybe it was a neighbor. The real estate agent had mentioned there were other tenants in the building, but it would be hard to prove it with everything she'd seen so far.

She swung the door open a couple of inches and placed her foot behind it to prevent it from being shoved open. It was a skill Rhoda taught her while her father showed her how to use her shoulder and body weight to force a door open once someone answered. A well-dressed, middle-aged woman stared back at her through the small opening.

"Mrs. Van Camp," she greeted her mother's long-time friend.

"Nala, aren't you going to invite me in?"

Manners forced her to swing the door wide even though she had no clue why her mom's friend would show up. Perhaps they had made plans to go somewhere after lunch. "Sure, come in. There's no furniture."

Her mother smiled at her friend. "Beverly, did you knock out that chunk of wood I had holding the building door open?"

Well, that explained how Mrs. Van Camp got in.

"I did."

"Good."

She smiled at the woman who had always bought whatever Nala had sold through her childhood years, from overpriced wrapping paper to cookies. "What brings you to my office?"

Max gave a bark, making her think he was protesting the use of *my* as opposed to *our* office. The last thing she needed was psychic messages from the dog that would convince her mother she truly had gone around the bend because of failing to marry and produce children at the optimum time.

Mrs. Van Camp put one hand up to her mouth as if to shield her words. "It's a personal matter."

"Oh, I can go into the other room if you need to speak to my mother." She turned to do so when the woman placed a hand on her arm.

"Oh no, sweetie. I came to see you since you now have a PI office and you already have a mascot." She nodded in Max's direction.

Nala wasn't too sure how the idea of mascot would go over, but Max sat up as if posing for a dog food commercial and wagged his tail. Her first client, although she was suspicious of the woman's actual need for assistance. "What can I do for you?"

"I think," she hesitated and glanced back in Gwen's direction. "It's Marvin, my husband."

"Yes, I met him. What about him?" The man always struck her as mild-mannered and under the thumb of his wife, which explained why she and her mother were such tight buds.

"Yes. I was wondering if you might, ah…" Mrs. Van Camp's skin reddened as she tried to explain.

Her mother called from her place on the pop-up stool. "Marvin is running around. Beverly needs pictures to stick it to him. Find out who the floozy is."

The woman in front of her deflated a little as she mumbled, "I hope it isn't anyone I know."

Her first instinct was to assure her Marvin wouldn't do such a thing, but that wouldn't be the proper PI response. "Okay. I'm going to record our interview on my cell." She stepped over to her purse, which was near her discarded ziti sitting on her own stool. She handed the pan to her mother. "You guard this while I do the interview."

Max sighed and flopped back to the floor, attesting his interest in her interrupted lunch.

"Okay, got it. Let's go into the inner office for privacy." She opened the door and ignored her mother's indignant huff.

Beverly walked in, and Max shot in after her. Nala closed the door behind her. "What makes you think your husband is stepping out on you?" She couldn't even form words like *tomcatting* or *screwing around* when it came to someone who had played the role of a jovial pseudo-uncle most of her life.

Mrs. Van Camp paced the small office, detailing unexplained absences, new clothes, and large cash withdrawals. It all sounded suspicious. "Did you ask him about any of this?"

"No. I didn't want to know that he…" A sob caught in her throat as she forced herself to continue, "…was tired of me."

Nala patted her pockets for a tissue but came up empty. "Ah." Her desire to reassure the woman struggled with her need for more information.

Ask her if she brought something of his I could smell? Max whispered.

OMG. The dog was telling her what to do. What next? "I'll need some addresses, such as his work, any place he claims he might be at, but you suspect he isn't."

After about ten minutes of listening to details, she'd calmed down enough about Max's interference until he did again.

Ask her if his clothes smell different.

Not too surprising, the dog focused on smell. Many forensic techs solved crimes using the tiniest clues. "Notice any unusual odors on his clothes?"

"If you mean lipstick or perfume, there was nothing." She held up one finger. "One day he came home smelling like Italian food."

"This is significant?"

"Yes, he hates Italian food. I'm the one who loves everything Italian. For a while, I even wanted to go to Italy, eat the food, visit the sites, and dance in the moonlight."

It interested her that Mrs. Van Camp had such a dream. "Why didn't you?"

"Marvin is afraid of flying anywhere."

"It makes sense that you never went, then."

"I may never get to Italy."

The statement ended in a wail that had her mother opening the door and entering to enfold her friend in her arms. "Don't worry, Beverly, the settlement you get will be more than enough to send you to Rome."

Her mother might know more than she was letting on. Perhaps she'd seen Marvin with another woman and asking her friend to call on Nala was just another way to break the awful news.

This wasn't what she thought being a PI would be like. She never expected to be personally involved with her clients, either. The sound of a metal pan hitting the floor drew her eyes to the open door. A quick survey of her inner office determined that Max was nowhere in sight. There would have to be some ground rules set for her *oh too smart* canine who even now was gulping down her lunch.

MAX PRESSED HIS nose against the car window, smearing the glass. He did this three times before he turned back to Nala and announced, "Look, I made a face."

"Yes, I see." She shifted in the uncomfortable vinyl seat and stared at the large building across the street. Originally, it had been a Masonic Lodge but now served as an arts center and reception rental spot. She couldn't figure out why Marvin went inside. At least, she hoped it was Marvin Van Camp she followed. The man drove a white sedan with no distinguishing scratches or dents. It was neither very new nor very old, which meant it looked like more than half of the cars on the road. Worse, Marvin resembled most men over forty, going bald in the back and thick around the middle. When he left his office, he had on khakis and a button-down shirt. She assumed she had tailed the right man.

A horrible possibility bloomed into existence. What if she had followed the wrong person on her first day on the job? It had been a while since she'd seen Marvin. It could have been six, maybe eight months ago. "What if he lost weight? Shaved his head? Got a spray tan?"

Max paused with his nose art to glance at her. "You should have asked for a photo."

"Lucky me. I have a know-it-all dog. Why didn't you tell me this before Mrs. Van Camp left?"

"I was more concerned about the scent factor. With the right smells, I could pretty much wrap this case up with one sniff."

"Maybe. I haven't seen any proof of your much-vaunted skills yet. You could just be all talk."

"Hah, you haven't given me anything to...*bark! bark! bark!*"

Max pushed his paws against the window, all but blocking a tiny section of the window.

Nala leaned sideways to see around her large dog. Most of the window was foggy, but in a small clear rectangle she could see Marvin Van Camp walking to his car with his hands in his pockets and smiling. The cocky saunter assured her it was Marvin. Her father commented that the man walked as if he were a much bigger deal than he was. She used her telephoto lens to bring the image in more. Just when she was ready to take the shot, something black blocked her angle.

A knock on her roof sounded throughout her car. Max barked wildly, throwing himself at the window. A deep voice sounded near the driver's side. "Police. Could you roll down your window, please?"

Police. What could the police want? She'd only been in the two-hour parking spot a little over an hour. She rolled down her window, remembering to be on her best behavior. Her father reminded her often that so many people were rude to the police that anyone using their best manners usually got out of a ticket. Although, there was no reason for a ticket. She rolled down her window and put on her best innocent expression that had served her well in high school and in some staff meetings.

"How can I help you, Officer…?" Her eyes looked for the name tag that would be pinned to his chest. Make that his very impressive chest. He must work out, and the uniform fit him like a glove. She managed to move her eyes up to his face, which wasn't bad either. His smirk announced he knew she was ogling him.

"Goodnight."

"Good night to you, too." She was ready to motor up her window, thinking it was peculiar the man had tapped on the car to wish her a good evening. Maybe the man was trying to interact with his community.

Speaking of cars, she peered around the officer just in time to see Marvin bump out of the parking lot and into a side alley. "Oh, snickerdoodles!" Her mother had caught her cursing after wiping out on her bicycle and demanded her father do something about it. Her father had counseled her to use the names of some of her favorite cookies when she felt the urge to curse. That way she could curse freely, if only in her mind, without her mother being the wiser. His suggestion had worked so well she seldom cursed now, except in cookie names. "Ah, I need to go now."

An elderly woman on the stoop of a small house stared in their direction. It was hard to be low key with a policeman at your car door. She made her way carefully down the steps and to the curb to yell across the street. "Aren't you going to arrest her and her demon dog?"

Max, who had calmly watched without a sound once she rolled down the window, made a questionable *yip* at being called demon dog.

The officer turned back to the woman on the curb. "I got this, ma'am. You can go back inside."

The woman stayed on the curb, crossed both arms, and directed a pleased smile her way. Once the officer turned back, she noticed his name label read *Goodnight*. Oh, now it made sense. He was telling her his name. I bet that went over well in bars. *Hi, I'm Goodnight.* Wait a minute. She remembered her father joking about a new officer called Goodnight. Said he was a war veteran or something. This had to be him.

"Officer Goodnight." She felt some confidence, knowing the man could be almost as much of a rookie as she was. "Did the lady on the curb call you about me and my demon dog?"

Max whimpered as if to say. *Stop with the demon label.*

"She did. Reported someone near her home with a dangerous dog that was making her and her cat anxious."

"If her cat could see Max from inside the house, then it has excellent vision. I'm not sure why he would be making the cat upset since he's in the car in a public parking place."

"All true. You'll get no argument from me. I still need to see your license, registration, and proof of insurance." He held out his hand.

Nala had to dig through her overstuffed purse to locate her wallet. "It's in here. Just a minute, I need to pull out some things. She pulled out her weapon and placed it on the console.

Goodnight stepped back from the car. "You have a gun."

The woman across the street put her hands around her mouth. "What's going on?"

"Yes. I need it for my job. I have a permit to carry a concealed weapon. My father had me on the range when I was nine. I'm an excellent shot." Her hand wrapped around something large and rubbery. She pulled it out before even considering what it might be. Good heavens, it was the vibrator Karly gifted her with. Embarrassed at the gift, she'd shoved it in her bag and forgotten about it.

Officer Goodnight had moved back to the car window and shook his head when he spotted the vibrator. "I don't want to know."

"Good, because I'm not telling you." Her fingers encountered the rounded edges of her wallet. "I found it."

"Great. Not too sure what might come out of that bag next."

The registration and insurance form were easier to locate since they were clipped to the visor. She handed him her license, and he read the name aloud. "Nala Bonne. Say, you aren't related to Captain Bonne?"

"He's my father."

The officer's demeanor changed from friendly to stiff and no nonsense in a heartbeat. She might have even called his previous behavior bordering on flirty. "I'm sorry to bother you, but we must respond to all calls. Can I ask you what you were doing with the camera?"

"It's mine, and I was taking a picture of the Masonic Lodge for my architecture class." She wasn't even sure if anyone offered an architecture class, but there were several colleges in the metro area so odds where one would. She didn't mention she was a private investigator because despite meeting basic requirements and taking online security classes, she hadn't received her card and license in the mail, yet.

"Okay. Makes sense. You'd probably get a better photo outside the car."

"Yeah, right." She'd have to take a picture of the building and catch up with Marvin later. If not today, then she'd have to start over tomorrow. Her hand passed over the gun and vibrator to grab the camera.

She stepped out of the car and aimed it in the direction of the building. With the telephoto lens on, all she would get was a window. Cradling the camera in her bent arm, she unscrewed the telephoto lens and turned her back to Goodnight so he wouldn't ask her about the lens.

"Hey! Stop!" The sound of the officer's shouted command had her pivoting to see what was the matter. Max had taken advantage of her open door and jumped out. Even though he was a large, dark dog, there was nothing threatening about him, but try to tell that to someone who didn't know him.

"Don't shoot him!"

"I wasn't going to. It's just, that, ah, he has something of yours."

Max pranced around the car carrying the oversized pink vibrator in his mouth. He acted as if he were proud of himself.

"You might want to put up your gun before he picks that up."

"I'm on it." She shoved the gun in her purse before she turned back to Max and pointed to the ground. "Drop it."

Instead of dropping it at her feet, he chose to drop it at Officer Goodnight's feet. Could her day get any worse? "Um." He bent over to pick up the vibrator from the knob end and offered it to her. "Here's your, uhm, property and have a nice night."

His cheek twitched as he tried to hold back a laugh and hurried to his patrol car. The woman across the street had disappeared into her house, probably to call for backup.

Chapter Five

NALA THREW THE vibrator onto the floor in the backseat. "We might as well head home and plan out tomorrow."

Max twisted his head to peer into the back seat. "It tasted funny. Yuk! Not sure, how anyone could chew on that."

"Why did you get out of the car? You don't do that when dealing with the police."

"You mentioned your father is a cop."

"That's different."

"How?"

"He's my dad."

"I was trying to help."

"I'm afraid to ask." She started her compact car, checked her side mirror for traffic and pulled out into the empty street.

"The cop was hot for you. Pheromones don't lie."

"You can tell this just by sniffing the air."

"I can."

The idea of bringing a dog along to those single mixers Karly insisted on them attending together might be useful. It always seemed like she got the signals wrong. Maybe it wasn't so much the signals, but more whenever she liked a guy, he didn't return the favor. When she thought someone was super creepy, like the man who dressed like a Ken doll, then that person would follow her around all night trying to get her number.

"What was the idea of playing fetch with the vibrator?"

"Vibrator?"

"Never mind." She wasn't sure she could explain to a dog that humans often turned to rubber and batteries for affection since it appeared so scarce in the human form.

Max glanced up at her as he spoke. "I thought I could get the two of you on friendlier terms with an old-fashioned game of keep away. Who doesn't love to play keep away?"

"Me."

"Yeah, I noticed. Can I give you some advice?"

"No, I refuse to take dating advice from a dog." She switched on the car radio just in case Max decided to offer advice.

His voice somehow made itself heard above Madonna singing "Papa Don't Preach."

"I know you're trying to shut me out. That woman calling the police wasn't my fault."

"You're right." Her phone rang before she could say anything else. She'd like to blame everything on Max, but it had been a series of events that added up to a huge fubar. She turned down the radio and touched the steering wheel control that answered her phone. "Hello."

"Nala, it's your father."

"I know, Dad. I recognize your voice. I'm not sure what Officer Goodnight said, but…"

"Goodnight? What are you talking about? I called because the alarm is going off on your building. I was checking to see if you were inside."

"No, I'm in my car with Max."

"Good. Don't go to the building. Enjoy your time with Max. Have I met him?"

"Not yet, but you will. Bye, Dad."

"What's this about Goodnight?"

"Bye." She hung up the phone, knowing she hadn't avoided the conversation, only delayed it.

A traffic light blinked red, forcing her to stop as she considered her destination. Whatever Marvin Van Camp was doing at the Masonic Lodge had to be part of the mystery. He could have been attending a meeting. He could be a Mason. It should be easy enough to inquire. Weren't Masons supposed to be secretive or were their rites a secret? Still, if you build a huge building in the middle of town, you couldn't be all that hush-hush.

The dashboard clock read 7:45, which meant Marvin was probably on his way home. Even though this was her first official case, the possibility that it might be a put-up job did occur to her. Let's make up something for little Nala. It made her feel all of six and wearing her Scout beret. Should she try to pick up Marvin's trail or investigate her building?

The loud blare of a siren forced her decision. "Okay, Max, it's back to the office, which I hope is still there. I barely scraped off the first layer of disuse and dust from the floorboards."

Two sharp barks announced what she assumed were agreement. A well-placed paw lowered the passenger window for Max to lean out and howl at the departing fire truck. When the light turned green, she accelerated in the direction of the truck, aware it couldn't be heading to her building since it sat several miles away in the downtown area.

"Stop that!" She pushed on the German shepherd currently serenading the city. A mini-van full of young children pointed and grinned at Max, only egging on her pooch. "I'm beginning to see how you ended up in the pound." She shouted the words to be heard over the noise.

The howling stopped abruptly, and Max pulled his head in and gave her a hurt look complete with liquid brown eyes. "Now, that was just mean."

"Yeah, it was. Sorry." Did she just apologize to a dog? When had her life taken a turn into crazy town? Her mother would have probably said it was when she broke up with Jeff, the promising surgeon. Mom never went out with him and never experienced how rude he could be to anyone he thought beneath him, which was almost everyone. She shuddered just thinking about the man.

"I stopped." Max poked her shoulder with his long, wet nose. "Don't go all dramatic on me."

"It wasn't you. It's…"

Frantic barking interrupted her explanation as a truck zoomed by on her left with a large dog riding in the bed. Max pressed against the windshield and barked wildly until the truck was out of view.

At least, it had stopped her from explaining a failed romance to her dog. That would have been a big mistake. While most pet owners did talk to their pets, they never worried about their pets spreading gossip later. So far, Max only seemed to talk to her, but he had talked to other people. With the result being that he ended up at the pound. It made her wonder why he even chose to speak.

"Ah, Max, what were you saying to the dog in the truck?"

He hung his head. "How embarrassing. I got sucked in. It was more attitude than anything else. The big bad dog was busy trying to get everyone to look at him, which I did. He symbolized freedom and power."

Nala didn't quite get if the dogs spoke actual words or broadcasted their feelings, but thought it might be the latter. "Why would you envy a dog whose owner doesn't even care about his basic safety? He could fall out of the truck. Not to mention being cold, hot, or rained on. That dog represents irresponsibility and neglect. He barked all that other stuff to make himself feel better about his place in the world."

Max stared through the front windshield. "Yeah, that sounds about right. Watch out for that scooter."

"What?" She swerved as a bright yellow scooter cut into her lane from the shoulder of the road. "Kids." She muttered the word to herself as her heart raced. Two seconds slower response and she would have hit them. "Thanks for warning me."

"It's my job."

Really, she was never clear on what a dog's job was besides making a single person appear less pathetic. On the other hand, too many dogs put a person smack dab back in crazy town. "What is your job?"

"You don't know?" Max turned and stared at her. "Karly didn't explain?"

If it involved her animal-rescuing friend, then the job might be to start some sanctuary for elderly poodles that their owners had abandoned. Most people didn't like to stick around to the very end. Too painful watching a playful pup turn into an arthritic hound. "Nope. Maybe you should."

"It could be a secret mission. I might be a spy dog."

"If you don't know if you're a spy dog, you're not. I'd say it's safe to tell me what it is."

Max huffed and gave a slobbery bluster. "That's what was missing from my life before, a mission. As mostly a German shepherd, I have a long heritage of dogs working to aid humanity. Granddad served in the war in Germany crawling across enemy lines. Mom was a bomb-sniffing dog while Dad aided in capturing dangerous criminals."

"Sounds impressive. Karly told me you had no clear bloodlines, which would probably mean you don't know your own relatives. As for the war, that would have been over seventy years ago, which is way too long."

"I meant Great-grandpa."

She eased onto the on ramp for the trek back to her office. "You're making this up."

"Why not? People make up stories about being related to royalty and celebrities. Why can't I?"

Her first urge was to insist the stories about being related to royalty was real, but she had her doubts. Darcy at the Laundry Tan and Nails insisted she was a cousin to the late Princess Diana. "Yeah, I guess they do it to feel important. And you? What's your excuse?"

"Same. I see my image in the mirror, and I try to envision a history that doesn't involve me being chased from my home with a crucifix. I know what I know, but the rest of my family could have been noble."

Cars and semi-trucks flew by making it hard to converse, but she still managed. "I understand, more than you might think. So, what about that mission thing?"

Max turned his head as a sedan with two Labradors in the back edged up beside her. "*Bark. Bark. Bark.*"

Not only had he changed the topic, but he changed the language, too.

Chapter Six

EMERGENCY LIGHTS GLARED in the approaching night as Nala slowed the car, trying to stare past the huge bulk of the fire engine. A thin trail of white smoke reached into the sky denoting the fire was no more. An ambulance lingered nearby, making her wonder if anyone had been in the building. A memory of the cute guy she met in the hallway crowded into her mind. She couldn't remember if he said he lived there or had an office there. Either way, he could have been endangered. A police officer waved at her to move on, mistaking her for a nosy onlooker as opposed to someone who had an investment in the building.

Right in front of her building were several open spaces, except they all had signs warning about the possibility of being towed. It must have been a loading area in the past. The area didn't have a wealth of street parking any way, but it was better than paying an arm and leg to park in one of the garages her father referred to as the perfect setting for a mugging. You'd think this late there would be some street parking, but maybe other people heard you got ripped off not only by entering the garage, but once inside too.

"Looks like we are going to have to park on the next street."

After driving two blocks in the opposite direction, Max spotted a place. "Over here. The SUV with the Dalmatian."

A white SUV at the curb did have a black and white spotted dog staring out the back window. "It's not moving."

"Watch."

The dog who had been standing suddenly sat as the brake lights flashed, and the car moved out.

"See." Max shot her an *I told you so* look as she pulled into the recently vacated space.

Weird, but right now she wanted to get to her office. Nala pulled in, shifted into first gear before withdrawing her keys from the steering column and attempted a firm countenance. "You stay here. I will only be gone a few seconds."

A sharp bark greeted her statement. When that had no effect, Max spoke. "Are you kidding me? Some do-gooder will come by and break your window because they saw a dog trapped in the car. Don't you get on the internet? It's a thing now."

Well, she had heard of some cases. "They only did that because it was hot, and the dog had been in there a long time."

"How do you know that? They may have felt like breaking a car window and used the dog as an excuse. What if a PETA member wandered down the street and saw me gasping out my last breath?" Max hunched his shoulders forward, allowed his head to droop, and let his tongue hang out.

"Enough." With the dog's acting skills, she might end up with a cruelty to animals charge. Worse yet, Max might end up back at the shelter where he couldn't be guaranteed another sympathetic owner or even life. She motioned to the shepherd. "You can come, but let's keep a low profile. If Dad said not to come, then it is a good bet he's here."

"Got it." He jumped out and joined her on the street.

Leash. She needed one. There was a county leash law. She'd

bought all the dog supplies yesterday and remembered leading Max to the office on a leash. When he had the lead on, he pretended to be choking, so she took it off with the promise he wouldn't run away. The needed leash must still be in the office. Great.

She slipped her glittery belt out of her belt loops with the intention of using it as a makeshift leash. Max backed up a few steps.

"Um, not that. Don't like the idea of being hauled around on a lead, but that…"

"Come on, it's only for a brief time. We duck in and ask a few questions, then leave."

"What about the other dogs?"

"There aren't any. Remember this morning. This is an office building that hardly anyone uses. No reason for there to be any dogs hanging around."

"Yeah. I'm not a fan of the sparkly belt, especially on me."

"Totally understand. I'm not that big of a fan, either."

Max appeared confused as she looped the belt around his collar. "It's for the preschoolers. I was supposed to dress in bright, cheerful colors. Glitter made me more of a fairy tale princess in their eyes. Once I get the office set up, I'll hit the thrift shop for less distinctive clothing. It would be easy for someone to spot me in my school bus adorned sweater."

Max didn't respond, which either meant he had no opinion or hadn't seen the sweater yet.

They continued walking past a man slumped against the building, drinking from a paper bag-clad bottle. He muttered in a hoarse voice that hinted at years of chain smoking and whiskey. "Hey, girlee."

Nala scooted closer to Max, glad she'd decided to bring him. If she was going to be a private eye, then she needed to toughen herself to the seamier aspects of the city.

The man pushed to a standing position and lurched after them. "How about a kiss, sweetie?"

Where was her pepper spray? She dipped her hand into her purse to feel for the cylinder as her heart kicked into double time. Hairbrush, tissues, mints, she could locate everything but what she needed. If she kept moving, she was only steps away from first responders.

In her search, she had dropped the lead. Max whirled around and confronted the man in a menacing tone. "Take a hike, buster, before I rip off your face!"

The intoxicated man backed off and darted down the street in a shambling manner.

"Thanks. You know you could have just bit him."

"No thanks. I don't go around putting my mouth on just anything. I have standards." He lifted his nose up.

Nala bent to grab the lead and decided not to mention drinking out of the toilet bowl since Max had saved her from an uncomfortable situation. Once they reached the corner, she could see the yellow slickers of the fire department members as they rolled up their hoses. It must mean the fire was over and they were packing up to leave. All she needed to do was to pretend to be walking her dog through the neighborhood.

Her eyes roamed over the various rescue workers. She needed someone young, not so grizzled by their job or nosy citizens. Not too inexperienced, either, since they would be anxious to follow the rules.

Before she could decide, one of them pushed their fire hat back, revealing a feminine profile. The woman nodded in her direction. "Nice dog. I used to have one like that."

"Yeah, he's pretty special." It was the opening she needed. "I appreciate you putting the fire out."

Another rescue employee walked by and grinned at her. "That's what we do. Hence the name."

The woman gestured at the departing man. "Ignore Barton. There wasn't all that much to put out. It was started at the wooden exterior doors triggering the fire alarm. Hopefully, the owner will put in steel doors now."

"Maybe." She didn't know what else to say. At this point, she should just walk on and vanish into the night as if a mysterious stranger or superhero. Yep, that's what she'd do. "Thanks for your service." Max added a bark.

A familiar voice cut across the chaos that accompanied most rescue scenes. "Did I hear a dog?"

While she expected her dad to be here, encountering him wasn't something she wanted right now. Nala lengthened her stride, hoping to reach the area not lit up by emergency lights. Max had no issue keeping up courtesy of four legs, but it didn't stop him from complaining.

"What's with the jog? I thought we were investigating. It's hard to do that when I can't put my nose down to sniff. I'm not a bloodhound you know."

"What does being a bloodhound have to do with it?"

She slowed to a walk, feeling a stitch in her side. Watching exercise shows with a hunky instructor wasn't quite the same as going to the gym. Her previous job, which consisted of squatting a great deal and rocking boo-boos away in her oversized rocking chair wouldn't serve her here. Different skill set needed, possibly running to make fast getaways.

"Bloodhounds can pick up a scent in the air. Don't even have to put their noses to the ground. They can follow a suspect in a car traveling at twenty-five miles an hour."

Nala glanced down. "How do they do that?"

"Not sure. Bloody never explained that to me. They can also track a trail over twelve days old. No other dog can."

"Impressive. So Bloody told you all of this?"

"Yep."

"You met him where?"

"The pound. He had some excellent skills and a few bad habits, such as ripping furniture apart to get to a mouse. Don't most people want a mouse-free house?"

"Yes. It was probably the furniture-free house they objected to."

They had almost reached the dark area. How ironic that darkness served as sanctuary. Maybe she had gone over to the dark side. There was a good chance that most of her tailing work would occur at night. During the day is when most folks went to work and assumed life as usual. The night was when things went a little crooked.

"Nala, is that you?"

Dad. She'd almost made it. Indecision froze her in place, but Max bumped up against her and asked, "Who's that?"

"My father."

"Is he mean?"

"No."

"Beats you?"

"Good heavens, no."

"Then why are you acting so weird?"

"Ah, it's hard to explain."

"As hard as a talking dog?"

Good question. She'd never tried to explain her complicated

relationship to anyone. As a child, she idolized her father and tried to be just like him. As the only child, she worked hard to be her father's little soldier while maintaining her role as her mother's little princess. Any therapist would have a field day with her. As an eager-to-please child, her goal had to have been not to displease either of them, but that wasn't doable.

"Probably not."

Max glanced over his shoulder. "He's big. Makes me wonder if you're the runt."

"Hush. I don't want to deal with both of you tonight." A sharp bark greeted her reply, which she had decided meant a type of agreement.

She pasted a smile on her face and turned. "Dad, imagine seeing you here."

He grunted as his brows came together into a V shape. "I distinctly remember telling you not to come down."

Her normal reaction would be to apologize. Max nudged her hand. He'd have no trouble asking why her dad was here.

Good counter. Wait, I'm being coached by a dog. Still, it worked. "So, what are you doing down here?"

"When something involves my little girl, I'm there. Your mother already told me the neighborhood was sketchy."

"It's not that bad."

"Some homeless guy was trying to burn his way into the building so he wouldn't have to sleep in the doorway."

"What makes you think it was a homeless guy? It could have been arson, even someone hoping to burglarize the place."

"Yeah, like that makes it better. A passing motorist called it in. She saw some guy starting a fire. It triggered the building alarm too. Not the first time, a homeless person started a fire to stay warm and it got out of control."

"It's summer." The season had descended upon Indianapolis with a vengeance, keeping both the temps and humidity high. It wasn't uncommon to reach triple digits by July.

"You're right, which makes a fire unneeded unless he was trying to cook something. Who knows? Some of the homeless people aren't the sharpest knives in the drawer." He slapped her on the back. "You're a smart one. We could have used you on the force, instead of you doing this private eye thing."

Before she could explain the reason, she needed to try it, her father continued talking.

"At least it's summer. You can try it and get it out of your system before school starts back. You didn't actually quit your job?"

She knew what he meant. "No, I figured I'd see how things worked out. I still have two months left to give my resignation. I could resign right before school starts, but that is kinda a jerk move. I have the office on a monthly rental basis, which is a little higher, but I figured it was the smarter option." Her natural caution kept her from cutting all her safety nets. After all, she didn't want to move back in with her parents if the agency didn't make it.

"You know, there's always a place for you at the academy."

Even in the dim light, she could see a speculative gleam in his eyes. The one thing she could say for her mother was she never expected her daughter to follow her into the interior design field.

"I'll keep that in mind." Nala didn't add she'd also keep in mind the long hours, bad press, and unreasonable demands made on the police. While she admired her father for the job he did, she preferred something a little more low-key and on her own terms, something where she didn't have to deal with parents who spun fantasies about their children being the next Olympian or president while ignoring their tendency not to play well with others.

If she stayed in the business long enough, some angry wife might have her tailing the grown-up version of her demon seed student who used the sharp edges of metal trucks as his weapon of choice.

THE FLICKERING EMERGENCY lights lit up the area around them, but darken the shadows around the buildings in contrast. Toby's cell mate had shared that tidbit. The man joked about hiding in plain sight only a few feet from the police in a convenient shadow. Still, he'd ended up in prison, so it hadn't worked all that well.

Toby kept his breaths slow and measured as to not attract notice. There was that girl and her dog again. The mutt was looking straight at him. Its ears pitched forward while the girl conversed with a tall man with ramrod posture. Probably a cop or possibly military. They tended to carry themselves with a coiled tension, ready to spring into action at any moment.

His plan hadn't been to burn down the building, but burn out the area with the lock. All he wanted to do was loosen the door enough for him to get inside. Still, even he knew enough that using a blow torch around the lock would get him behind bars faster than he could blink. His intention was to make it resemble a small fire at the foot of the door, the type a budding pyromaniac might start. The kerosene-soaked rags and wood flamed up and started to char the door when he heard sirens. He shot away from the building and across the street into a narrow alley between two buildings and waited.

The sirens blasted past the street, not even stopping. How could he have forgotten that sirens were going off all the time in the city?

Everything from heart attacks to car wrecks would send the first responders tearing around in the city. Just when he was going to investigate how his fire was going, the grinding brakes of a fire engine sounded as it turned the corner.

Toby swore. Who would have thought the old building had a fire alarm system? It was decrepit when Gabe used it for his office.

As criminals went, Gabe had flare. He came up with opening an office so people who wanted a job done could contact them as if they were regular businessmen. No alley meetings or waiting around in dive bars for their clients to show. They even had business cards printed up with a burner phone number that couldn't be traced with script letter announcing *No job too small.*

Vindictive spouses, burned partners, even other thieves walked through the door and explained what they needed stolen. Some even gave them keys or security codes, which made the job that much easier. The obvious question was why they didn't do it themselves. Gabe put it down to they didn't want to risk being caught. Money changed hands without names being exchanged just in case.

You can't tell what you don't know, which was Gabe's parting sally whenever a client asked about the no-name policy. It worked, at least for Gabe, on their last job together. His glib-tongued partner tucked the emeralds Toby had liberated from the safe into his tuxedo and bid the hostess goodbye, and then Gabe slid into his rented Porsche and took off.

Despite his skills with alarm systems and safes, his getaway was foiled by a small yappy dog. The little hairball not only barked but sunk its teeth into his pants as he tried to escape out the window, he had opened for such a purpose.

With a party in full swing, people should have ignored the barking, but Napoleon's owner wasn't the type. When the police arrived, she was upset he might have damaged her precious dog, which meant they hadn't discovered the missing emeralds yet. He always closed the safe and put back any obvious effort to hide it such as a painting or rug. It might be months before someone checked for an expensive necklace or an important document. He even stole a will once and substituted a fake one.

He expected a slap on the wrist for breaking and entering, although his defense was the window was already open. Instead, his court-appointed lawyer arrived with a list of everything the Clampetts decided was missing from their home along with the emeralds. The list was two pages long and included such notable items as a four-foot Ming vase and a Gainsborough portrait. Gabe and Toby didn't deal in such items because it was almost impossible to walk out of a house with a three-foot vase or a landscape taller than he was. Could be the family's staff or relatives had helped themselves to a few things. More likely, they had been selling off stuff to support their lavish lifestyle.

What would have been strictly probation only ballooned into prison time. Gabe never contacted him. The burner number no longer picked up. He couldn't leave a voice mail since they didn't operate that way. Inside, he got a reputation for writing good letters for men who were romancing prison groupies. Desperate women who were willing to invest time in writing prisoners and putting money into their canteen account.

One of the grateful inmates, who was getting out, even promised to look up Gabe and get back to him. Word on the street was that Gabe died in a horrible car wreck. The former inmate had even managed to get into the building and made it all the way up to the third-story office. The faux leather furniture was gone along with any hint of the business conducted in the office.

Whoever owned the building was within his rights to remove the furniture and trash it. Still, that never answered the question whether Gabe died or only set it up to look like he had. Whatever happened had occurred right after Toby's incarceration, since he'd had an unwelcome visit from the person who hired them to steal the emeralds. About that time, he realized Gabe had double-crossed them both. He shook his head, considering the possibility, and watched the fire trucks leave.

The last police car left as did the tall man. He waited until the last tail light vanished into the dark.

Every now and then a hunch kept him out of harm's way. Gabe wasn't dead, he felt it. That meant the emeralds could be hidden in the building. They'd have to be taken apart and smuggled out of the country. Airport security being what it was a boat might be safer.

No cars, no police, the coast was clear. The street light next to the building stayed dark. Perfect. He was halfway across the street when he heard voices. What the—he froze in the middle of the street. Fortunately, there were no cars coming.

Underneath the non-working light stood a bearded guy and the girl with the dog. The canine gave a single woof and stared in his direction. Toby would have sworn his eyes gleamed red, but that was his imagination.

Act casual. He put his hands into his pockets and continued to walk across the street. Even managed a whistle. As he drew closer, the beast had the nerve to growl at him.

Both the man and girl glanced up in interest, which meant it was showtime. He weaved a little and managed a few choruses of "Elvira."

Toby staggered past them, but their voices still carried on the still night.

"There goes another drunk music lover," the man commented. "Not sure what's bringing out the crazies tonight."

"Yeah, I hear you," the woman agreed.

"He smells funny. Bad," another male voice interjected.

Strange, he'd only seen two people standing there, but there could have been a third.

The bearded guy spoke again. "Pardon me?"

There was a flurry of coughing. "Excuse me. Allergies sometimes screw with my voice."

"Ah, yeah. Understand. You said the man smelled bad."

"Phew! You couldn't smell him? Gross. Probably hasn't washed for days."

Toby stiffened, taking offense at the statement. He managed a shower the other day while at the Y. He'd slipped in when a member walked in, then made a quick turn to the locker room while the member chatted up the receptionist. Toby knew he didn't smell that bad, and the girl was lying, which made him curious as to why.

Chapter Seven

A BRIGHT ORANGE crushed velvet couch greeted her when she opened her office door the next day. "Of course, mother would send me this monstrosity."

Max leaped on it and laid down. "Ooh. Nice. I like it."

"It goes so well with your black hair. My mother has had this piece of furniture in the warehouse for the last decade. She and Emily, her co-designer, have tried to unload the orange sofa on various clients calling it cutting-edge, edgy, and hipster. So far, no takers. She even tried to give it to me when I moved out."

"Why did she get it, then?"

"Someone with blatant disregard for good taste ordered it. By the time it arrived, the client had cancelled the project, and the vendor refused to take it back. No massive surprise there."

She might as well see what other tidbits her mother decided she no longer needed in her warehouse. A bamboo and glass coffee table sat off to the side as if the movers had dropped it and ran. They were probably trying to get out before she arrived. The better question would have been how her mother even got into the building to begin with. Knowing her mother, she probably talked the super into letting her in on the strength of their blood relation. She could have even offered the super a discount at Posh Interiors.

If her mother ever decided to become a crime lord, her father would be in trouble big time. Not only would he refuse to testify against his wife, he wouldn't be able to outsmart her, either. Sometimes, Nala wasn't even sure why she tried to resist her mother's helpful efforts.

In the corner sat an ivory slipper chair that appealed, which made her wonder how it ended up here. It must have been part of a pair, and a client only wanted one. A rolled-up carpet rested against the corner. It might be interesting to see what rug people didn't want.

She pushed the interior door open to see what else might be hiding. A huge dark desk took up about a quarter of the room. The movers must have cursed up a storm moving that behemoth. Behind the desk was a top-of-the-line leather desk chair, which was no one's reject.

Nala moved around the desk to sink into the supple chair. It tilted, twirled, and moved easily across the wooden floor. It even had lumbar support and a massage unit. How great was that? Even better, the chair symbolized her mother's belief she could make a success of it, unlike her father who was holding a spot for her at the academy.

The sound of clicking dog nails meant Max had abandoned his love affair with the orange sofa. He strolled into the interior office and stopped. "That's a big deal desk."

"You think so?"

"Yep!"

"It's ginormous, much bigger than I need. On the upside, I probably won't need a filing cabinet right away with all this desk space. I should call mom and thank her."

A knock sounded on the exterior door. "Maybe I won't have to call. This could be her."

Nala moved to the entry and swung open the door, preparing to greet her mother only to be confronted with a non-descript woman of indeterminate age instead. "Hello, can I help you?"

The stranger's lips tried for a smile but failed. She held up a crumpled piece of paper. "I'm looking for the Nala Bonne Detective Agency. I met a man at the front who let me in and told me the agency was on the third floor. I didn't see any signs, but your door was the only one with lights inside."

Nala motioned to herself. "I'm Nala Bonne, and you've come to the right place. I just set up business and don't have my name on the door yet."

"Oh." The woman appeared disconcerted. "If this isn't a good time, I'll come back later."

Gwen Bonne may not have taught her daughter a great deal about business, but she did stress that people seldom came back, even if they wanted something. The sale had to be made immediately.

"Please come in. Have a seat." She gestured to the exterior office. The woman headed for the orange sofa now liberally decorated with dog hair. "Not there." She grabbed the woman's arm. "In my office, and I'll bring the dog hair-free chair with me."

As she carried the slipper chair behind the woman, she had the opportunity to observe the cut of her clothes. Expensive, hand tailored, conservative, and possibly too old for the wearer, unless she was a sixty-year-old woman who had managed to keep her skin wrinkle-free due to some pricey skin care regimen.

"Here we go," She lowered the chair to the floor and hurried behind her desk. What she needed was a calendar, notepad, or pen or something to look more professional. Otherwise, she'd have to record the meeting. While her previous client didn't mind, this one was looking for any reason to bolt. Max sat down outside the interior doorway, blocking the only escape route.

She smiled at the unknown woman and fiddled with her desk drawer, which she opened the tiniest bit. The flash of color caught her eye, and she opened it more. Inside she found a planner, blotter, notepad, and several pens. *Bless you, Mother.*

Pen in hand, she flipped open the notebook. "You don't mind me taking notes, Ms...." She waited for a name.

"Constance Bingham."

Her pen moved across the pad, writing the name and the date. It helped Nala to disguise the fact that she recognized the name of one of the most influential and wealthy families in the area. She'd never met Constance, had never seen a photo of her in the paper, but she did know she was the only daughter of a wealthy industrialist. She only knew this because about twenty years ago her father was involved in rescuing a kidnapped Constance.

Thoughts gathered and an inscrutable expression in place, she asked, "Okay, what can I do for you?"

"I want you to investigate someone."

"All right." That's what she did, but someone with Constance's money probably already had someone on payroll to do such things. "Why pick me?" It may not have been the best question to ask.

"It has to be discreet. I don't want anyone to know. It's about someone in my company." The woman cast a backward glance over her shoulder as if she expected an uninvited listener lurking.

"I'm nothing if not discreet."

"That's what my friend said."

Friend? Someone recommended her before she had even completed her first case. "May I ask who?"

"I'm not at liberty to say. Let's just say you came very highly recommended."

Even the recommendation was a mystery. One she'd solve. "Who do you want me to investigate?"

"Gordon Lansing, the current CEO of Bingham Industries. Technically, he works for me, but as of late I have my doubts."

Good, an easily researchable person, but would she be able to dig up the hidden information on the man? "What caused your suspicions?"

"Before, Gordon was pretty forthcoming with details about mergers and bottom lines. I usually attended all the stockholders' meetings, and sometimes he'd even come to the house to present me with the reports, usually at dinnertime."

"This concerns you how?" So far, Nala hadn't been able to discern any questionable behavior on Gordon's part.

"Most of the time, I'd invite him to stay for dinner, which usually lasted a couple of hours. I didn't think much of this until I heard rumors that Gordon and I were dating. My father's secretary told me. Mary Broom. Anyhow, she has always been a bit of a mother to me since mine died. I insisted on keeping her around after my father's death."

The plot was thickening. "What did Mary say?"

"She asked me if I was dating Gordon. I told her no, which she said was good because the man was a snake in the grass. The board appointed him, not me. I assumed he was a good businessman, and we were always in the black until…"

"Until what?" Nala scooted to the edge of her seat as the story unfolded.

"Once I heard the tale about us dating, I told him what I heard. He laughed about it and said something about let's give them something to talk about, then tried to kiss me right in the office with the door open so everyone could see."

"It's obvious he wants people to think you're dating. To what purpose?"

Constance shook her head. "That's part of the reason I'm here. After that scene, I made it known in no uncertain terms that we had never dated nor would we in the future. The open door worked in my favor that time."

"Then what happened?" Her pen skimmed across the tablet as she made notes.

"He stopped bringing reports to the house, and has resorted to talking to me like I'm eight as opposed to twenty-eight in front of the board members."

That answered the age question. The woman was dressing too old for her age. "I'd think the talking down to you is a petty reaction to you refusing to date him."

"Maybe but it is more than that." She gestured to her face and torso. "I know good and well I don't drive men mad with desire. It's my money they lust after. Gordon is no different. When I made it clear I didn't welcome his intentions, he took a different approach to the money."

"How so?"

"The company is now leaking money in a thriving economy. Everyone else is making money except Bingham Industries."

"Is it a lot?" Everyone knew that businesses had their ups and downs.

Constance tapped her index finger against her temple. "It depends. In regard to a multi-national corporation, it isn't. Around ten thousand a day, more or less. That's loss only. I suspect Gordon is punishing me and helping himself. It might even be more. This is what he's reporting."

"Hmmm," Nala stalled, pretending to look thoughtful. She had no clue how to handle what could be possible embezzlement. Didn't the police or the FBI handle that type of stuff? "Have you considered a forensic accountant?"

"I have. Currently, Gordon is all buddy-buddy with the board members. They think he can do no wrong."

"Do you hold a controlling interest?"

"Our family does. I hold forty-five percent with my Aunt Ophelia holding six percent. Gordon has taken advantage of her spotty memory and convinced her he's my father, so she usually does whatever he says."

The case grew more and more complicated. "What is it you want from me?"

"Proof that Gordon is embezzling so I can take it to the board."

Nala didn't know the board but couldn't see any good coming from that. "Don't go to the board. Get your facts and go to the FBI. A crime is a crime. You don't need approval to investigate it."

Constance did not appear convinced. She pursed her lips and then sighed. "What if the company is truly losing money?"

"It might be time for a new CEO. Either way, it bears investigating."

"That's why I'm here. I'm hesitant to say anything to the board members since they'd call up their good buddy, Gordon."

"What about the accountant? I assume you have several accountants."

"We do. The head accountant was personally appointed by Gordon recently when Hazel retired. If Hazel were still working, I bet we wouldn't be losing money." Constance made an audible exhale. "I know you don't know me, but I'm not known for being bold or even business-minded. I got my master's in art history, which means I'm great at an art museum, but not much good anywhere else. For most of my life I've had no interest in Bingham Industries, but now I do. When I try to take part in the board meetings, I'm frozen out by all the good old boys who tell me not to worry my pretty little head. I need to nail Gordon to the wall to prove I'm worthy of being there."

Constance wrung her hands and shifted in the chair. She exhaled audibly and continued. "I wanted an intelligent woman to help. Someone who wouldn't be taken in by Gordon's surface polish. He's not at all how he pretends to be." Her voice swung up at the end of the sentence and wavered the tiniest bit as if it would break.

It may have been the longest speech the woman had ever made. "I take it this situation has alarmed you."

Constance's eyes fluttered shut, and she gave a small moan. "Terrorized would be a better description. When I get overwhelmed, I can't even think straight." Her eyes opened, and her two hands came together in a prayer-like gesture. "You've got to help me!"

"You convinced me. I'll need all the information you have on Gordon. Does Mary know his secretary? Better yet, does she have access to his social calendar?"

"She should since Gordon hired a showy blonde who is always asking Mary for help. I wouldn't be surprised if Mary made up the passwords."

What had seemed like an impossible task just got more doable. "All right, Ms. Bingham. I have homework for you. Draw up a list of who you think you can depend on and who is firmly in Gordon's pocket. Don't contact any of them, though."

"Why am I doing this?"

"Male embezzlers tend to work in groups, while women work alone." Fortunately, she got that tidbit from an online financial page.

She flipped her notebook closed. "I think I got what I need here." Nala stood and waited for Constance to do likewise.

The woman reached into her purse and withdrew a checkbook. She used the edge of the desk to write on, ripped out the check, and handed it to Nala. "Will that be enough to retain your services?"

Deep, slow breath, she coached herself. Act casual. Max raised his head and sent her a mental message. *Ask her if she brought something of his I can smell.*

"It will serve."

Ask her.

Max might not even let the woman leave until she asked, probably destroying all creditability. Nala cleared her throat, knowing she could lose the fastest twelve thousand dollars she had ever made. "I use my dog for trailing people. He's an excellent tracker. Would you possibly have something of Gordon's?"

Constance gave a light-hearted laugh. "I do. The fool left his sterling silver cigarette case at my house." She pulled a plastic bag from her purse, holding the silver case. "I found it after the scene at corporate headquarters. I knew when I saw it that it was his plan to return to get it. I don't allow any smoking at my house. I tried not to touch it. At the time, I wasn't thinking of using it to track anyone. It was more of an ick factor. My intentions were to return it to prevent him from thinking something was going on between us. I bagged it hoping to cut down on the cigarette smell. If it stunk up my purse, I'd end up throwing it away."

Max stood and walked to the desk. Nala took the bag Constance offered and opened it for the dog. The acrid smell of tobacco wafted out. He stuck his nose in it, grimaced, then coughed.

"My opinion, too. That's why I bagged it."

"We might be able to lift prints or even DNA from it." Nala

smiled at the woman as she walked around the desk. "Well, I need to get to work on your case." Which will be hard if you don't leave and let me call in every favor ever owed to me and a few that weren't. With any luck, one favor would involve fingerprinting.

As soon as the door closed, Max put his paws on the desk to examine the check. "Whoo doggy, that's some check."

"I should cash it before she changes her mind."

Chapter Eight

AFTER DEPOSITING THE check, Nala and Max went on an extensive search of the city for a spy shop. There were none. Even the high-end, electronics stores didn't have the surveillance equipment she needed. Something along the caliber of what super spy James Bond used, only it had to be real instead of fictional. Outside of La Margarita, she dialed Elvin Snopes. In the school yearbook, he received dual designation as *geekiest guy* and *most likely to shoot up the school.* Not too surprisingly, he went into a career of legal hacking. Companies asked him to find holes in the firewalls, anti-virus software, and networks they installed. Police departments and even the FBI had used him to break codes.

"Hello, sweetcakes."

Nala rolled her eyes. Elvin thought it immensely entertaining to call her sexist names such as babe and hot lips after her speech about demeaning name-calling in Public Speaking 101. Normally, she'd correct him, but today she needed his skill set.

"Hey, Elvin. I have a problem. It's something I know you can do. Not sure who else I can go to since it's a sensitive matter."

"Understand."

"Good. It needs to stay secret."

"I'm your man."

"Let me tell you what I need."

"No need. I'll be at your place at seven. Do you prefer red or white wine?"

She paused, unsure if she'd lost control of the conversation. She wasn't sure if they were on the same page. "No reason to come over. You can do it all on your computer."

"Cool. A real cyber geek. So, what exactly do you want me to do?" His voice took on a suggestive tone that caused Nala to pull the phone away from her ear and throw a bewildered look at the device. Max gave a sharp bark.

"ARGH. YOU ALMOST broke my eardrum. What was that for?" Elvin asked.

Nala placed the cell back to her ear and winked at Max. They were becoming quite a team. "Oh, that was Max. He's my new partner since I put out my private eye shingle. That's what I need your help for. I need you to look into someone's background. I can give you the name, address, social security number and all that. It may not be his own, though. If this works out, maybe I could throw more business your way."

"Only if you promise not to let your dog bark into the phone."

"So, how about it?"

"Have lunch with me."

"It wouldn't be a date."

"A business luncheon. It would do my street cred good to be seen with a babe." He chuckled, knowing the term would grate.

"Whatever. I'm getting ready to go into La Margarita and request an outside table since I have Max. You can meet me there and advise me on picking out surveillance equipment."

"It's a plan. It just might be my secret fantasy. See ya."

"Bye." She powered off the phone. "Never sure how to take the man, but he's the best at what he does. Maybe it's hard for the super intelligent to work well with the ordinaries."

Max charmed the waitress who brought him a bowl of water. Chicken and chorizo nachos tempted Nala, but she should wait for Elvin in case he wanted to share an appetizer. The iced tea helped to dissipate some of the summer heat. At least she wasn't covered with hair like Max.

Elvin came around the corner at a trot, causing his glasses to bounce on his nose. She waved just in case he failed to recognize her.

"Hey, there you are." He grinned and took a seat.

Max immediately stood up, gave Nala an impish look before sniffing Elvin. She did her best not to laugh as her hacker friend tried to push the dog away.

"Glad you could make it. I haven't ordered any food yet. I'll pick up the bill."

"My day keeps getting better and better. Could you call Rin Tin Tin off?"

"Max," she pointed to the ground, "sit." He did, which surprised her. Maybe the dog had been trained at some point.

The attentive waitress reappeared and handed a menu to Elvin, who ordered a mango margarita without looking at the menu. Nala decided to go with her first choice, the nachos.

Once the waitress left, Elvin pulled out his tablet, powered it up, and gave a small whoop. "They do have Wi-Fi!"

"Um, Elvin, you do realize public WIFI isn't secure?" Maybe she needed to rethink her use of her former classmate.

"Puh-lease, who do you think you're dealing with? I have cryptography software on all my machines. It's constantly scrambling any signals just in case we have any nosy sorts who hoped to check out some naughty pics." He wiggled his eyebrows on that comment. "It also confuses those who want to peek at my bank account or credit cards. No way, Jose."

Why didn't that make her feel better? Her expression might have telegraphed her uncertainty to her companion.

He mugged at her. "Why so glum?" He laughed maniacally as if he had told a hilarious joke, instead of repeating a tired movie quote A few outdoor diners stared at him.

"Stop it. You're attracting attention. Exactly what I don't want. A PI must stay low profile."

Elvin managed to stop laughing, but had to take a deep breath before he could speak. "If you don't want people to notice you, then ditch the dog."

A yip greeted that remark, letting them know what the canine thoughts were on the subject. "I can't get rid of Max. He helps me."

"How?" He pulled his glasses down to shoot her a mock serious look.

Elvin enjoyed being dramatic, using movie quotes, and a host of other irritating behaviors he thought made him endearing. It was easy to forget about his various mannerisms when she wasn't around him on a regular basis, but it was all starting to come back.

"He tracks people."

"In the city?" Disbelief sounded in his voice.

"It's possible."

He ignored her answer as he greeted the waitress who brought him his drink. "Hello gorgeous, where have you been all my life?"

She giggled before putting down the drink and rushing back to the kitchen.

"It's not fair to flirt with the waitress."

"Why is that? I'm unattached."

"It astounds me. The waitress has to be nice to you because she wants a good tip."

"Naw, she likes me."

His cocky manner grated. "Wanna bet? Five dollars?"

"Surely you could go a little higher than that." He lifted his right hand as if directing a choral ensemble. He kept moving it higher.

"How about this, lover boy? You do this job free if you don't get her number?"

"Sounds good." He put out his hand to shake. About the time Nala grasped his, he asked, "Wait. What happens if I do get her number?"

"You get paid, and you have her number. What else could you want?"

He gave her hand a firm shake. "It all seems fair, especially since you're going to lose." He waved the waitress over. "I just wanted to say how much I enjoyed being served by you." His eyes dropped to her name tag. "Teresa."

Nala held up one finger to get the flustered waitress's attention. "Please give me the bill since both meals are on me."

Teresa's eyes widened the tiniest bit, and she gave a short nod before moving to the next table.

"That was underhanded."

"No worse than making her think you were going to give her a big tip. She would have given you a fake number, anyhow. I didn't invite you here to pick up chicks. Come to think of it, you should be the one picking up lunch. Something about your street cred."

"Yeah, that reminds me." He pulled out his phone and snapped a photo of Nala. He peered at his phone and shook his head. "Your mouth is open. You look like a cross between a baby bird waiting to be fed and an opera singer."

She made a grab for his phone, which he held out of reach. He put the phone behind his back, but leaned slightly across the table, almost knocking over Nala's tea. When his head was almost touching hers, he whipped out the phone again for a selfie of the two of them. "That one was for my dying grandmother who can go on to her great reward knowing I have a woman to take care of me."

"Yeah, I bet. Delete it. Here I'll do it." She reached for his phone he hovered over. "You better not be doing anything."

"I'm linking your baby bird pic with your phone number. That way I'll always know when you're calling."

"That better be all you do."

He held up his hand with his thumb bent across the palm. "Scout's honor. Although, it wouldn't hurt to have a photo of the two of us show up on social media."

"Elvin." Her low, threatening tone had Max growling, too.

His jovial expression took an anxious turn. "Chill, you two." He handed the phone to Nala. "You delete it."

She stared at the picture of the two of them. Elvin was grinning, of course, but she looked good for an unexpected shot, even happy. Instead of deleting it, she handed the camera back. "It's not a bad shot. You can keep it."

"Great." He took back the phone and deposited it in his pocket. "Since I already posted it." At her look of outrage, he added, "Just joking."

"Do you honestly think we can work together with you always making jokes and fooling around? I'm not so sure."

Her chosen hacker choked a little on his drink, put it down, and coughed once before wiping his mouth with the back of his hand. "All you had to do was tell me to knock it off, like everyone else does. You never told me to knock it off before so I assumed you liked the entire act."

"I don't." She slumped back in her chair. "It exhausts me. You're not like this with the police, are you?"

"No! I only bring out my playful side for the ladies."

"Which totally explains why you're single."

"I don't see any ring on your left hand."

"Yeah and that's the way I like it. Are we going to talk business or just eat our Mexican food and leave?"

"Personally, I want to do both. Did you bring me the information?"

One of her stops had included a run by the copy place where she made the copies herself. Another thing she'd need for her office was a printer/copier combo unit. It wouldn't have to be big to keep her from making copy runs. The manila envelope contained all the information she'd gathered on Gordon. She handed it to Elvin. "This is all I have, but I want you to follow the trail carefully. Even though I knew nothing about this man before today, my instinct tells me something is up. Time is of the essence. If you could get me something in twenty-four hours, you'd be golden."

He pulled the papers and paged through them. "He's obviously a major business player."

"Or he wants us to think he is."

"Why do you say that?"

"Every photo I pulled up of him at various events is bad."

"Not everyone can take a gorgeous photo every time like moi." He patted his hand on his chest.

"I thought you were going to knock it off." She wrinkled her nose.

"Hey, I'm trying. It may not happen overnight. So, what do you mean by bad?"

She pulled the papers out of his hand and shuffled through them until she found the photo she wanted. "He's in the process of turning away from the camera. In all the photos, everyone else is posing for the picture, but it looks as if he's trying to escape. I'm hard pressed to know what he even looks like. All I get is tall, white, blond male from what little I see. He could almost be anyone. I had to call my client and have her explain in detail what he looks like."

"That's peculiar. Most of these important dudes want their photos taken. Strange he never wants to."

Nala held up one finger. "It makes me wonder why."

"He could be wanted somewhere for something."

"Yeah, I thought that, too, but working in plain sight isn't any way to hide from the law."

The waitress brought them their food and placed it on the table. Nala almost laughed when the woman ignored Elvin's attempt to flirt. They both dug into their food and ate silently.

Elvin waved his empty fork as he talked. "Makes me wonder about the camera shyness."

"Hmm, this is good." The chicken chorizo nachos were delicious and almost took all Nala's attention, but part of her mind processed the information. "I've been thinking about this on the way over here. Talked it over with Max."

A laugh escaped her lunch companion. "And you call me weird."

"I never called you weird. I called you annoying. Why wouldn't a person want to be photographed? What if Gordon isn't the multimillionaire he is purported to be?"

"You mean he's not Batman!" Elvin waved his hand as Nala opened her mouth to speak. "Before you say anything, I'll stop."

Not likely. She chose not to verbalize her thoughts. Instead, she slipped a loaded nacho to Max, who snapped it up. Her pooch nudged her leg for more. She picked off the jalapenos before offering them.

"I realize some people are motivated by money. Others by power and the majority by both. I want to know how this guy is wired. My client told me he attempted to romance her for her money. He thought she was some desperate spinster who would jump at an interested man. When she let him know emphatically that she wasn't interested, the company started losing money immediately."

Elvin tossed back his drink and gave his glass a mournful glance that had the waitress hurrying over and inquiring if he wanted another one. At his head bob, she hurried off.

"I hope you're not driving."

"Uber."

Lunch finished, Nala pushed her plate away and directed her gaze to her companion. "Have you been listening to a word I just said?"

"Which part? The part about your client being Constance Bingham? Or the part about when Gordon put the moves on her, she kicked him to the curb?"

"Yeah, that part. I didn't tell you who the client was."

"Oh, it wasn't a huge leap since you will have me hacking into the files of Bingham Industries, CEO."

Nala reached into her bag for her wallet when her fingers encountered the plastic bag that housed the forgotten cigarette case. She lifted the bag high enough for her companion to see it.

He leaned across the table and poked it with one finger, causing the bag to swing. "I wouldn't have taken you for a smoker. The cigarette case is so retro. As for the plastic bag, is that a girl thing?"

"No. Not my case. It does happen to have the fingerprints of Gordon Lansing. What I need is someone to pull and run them."

"I know someone."

"I suspected as much. Who?" She waved her free hand. "Never mind. All I need is accuracy."

"Got that. Can't be part of the bet, though. This guy charges."

"How much?"

"For me, he'll do it for the low rate of hundred and fifty."

"He must not like you very much. I'll send the money to your online account."

Elvin reached for the bag and laughed. He placed it on top of the papers. His phone chimed. "There's an Uber car close by. Time for me to get to work. It's been fun, Robin."

He stood and gathered up his tablet, plastic bag, and the manila envelope containing the Gordon Lansing info. As he turned to go, Nala yelled after him, "You're not Batman!"

He didn't bother to turn, leaving Nala the focus of some interested diners. Staying low profile would take much more work than she originally thought.

Chapter Nine

AFTER LUNCH, NALA drove to Posh Interiors. She needed a dog sitter since she intended to go to the mall for disguises. Some law allowed people to drag their pup almost anywhere and call it a companion dog. If a shop owner complained, the person could explain how the dog was necessary for mental health purposes, which most people wouldn't touch with a ten-foot pole. With that type of reasoning, she could get Max a medical or guide dog vest.

The one thing she did remember when people showed up in places that normally prohibited pets, people stared, commented, and remembered. She didn't need any of that when she went shopping for her disguise.

As she turned onto the street where Posh Interiors was located, she decided to tell Max about their destination. "We're going to see Momsy. She's the nice woman who gave you the breadstick. You two will be such good friends."

"Not the baby talk. Never cared for it. Suspect most dogs don't. So, are you off-loading me onto your mother?"

"Not off-loading. Allowing you to examine her business while I run to the mall."

"Yippee." Max's flat tone indicated his feelings.

"Hey, you told me yourself about what happens to dogs in cars."

"Yeah. Don't remind me."

"Mom has employees who will love you."

"Your mother has a company full of comfy couches and over-stuffed chairs of the large variety?"

"Well, yes." She already sensed Max would make himself unwelcome. "There'll be no jumping on the furniture. It's merchandise. The goal is to sell it to someone."

"Who wouldn't want a little dog hair? Gives it the homey feel." His lips pulled up into a canine smile.

"Plenty of people. What about people with pet hair allergies?"

"Faking it."

"Those who don't like hair on their divan."

"They need to loosen up before they have a stroke."

"Max." Her voice took a cajoling tone. "I need you to be on your best behavior. I'll bring you something from the mall."

"A giant pretzel?" His ears tented forward, awaiting her reply.

Odd. She would have expected a rawhide bone or a pig ear, but nothing about Max was ordinary. "Okay."

Yip. Yip. Owooooe.

"Here we are." She pulled into the lot loaded with high-end cars and steered away from the other cars whose owners would be convinced she was there to carjack them until they discovered she was really Gwen's daughter. Then she'd be precious. "We'll go in the service entrance."

"Not good enough for the front door?"

"It's not that. Some of the employees will be spinning fantasies of what the potential rooms or houses will look like. The tiniest distraction could cause a client to look away. Trust me. You are a distraction."

"It's my natural good looks."

"Twenty minutes with Elvin and you sound like him." Nala opened the unlocked back door to the store. Her father had mentioned this security breach more than once. Her mother waved it away by saying it was difficult with so many employees going in and out the door. They entered a narrow hallway that had several doors leading off from it. At the end of the hallway stood a knight in full armor.

Max pulled to a stop. "What do you have to do to get past the guard?"

"He's not a guard. Just a statue a client had to have until he realized his foyer was too small to accommodate it."

A door swung open, and Gwen popped out and looked around. "I thought I heard your voice and that man again. Where is he?"

Her lips twisted as she wondered how to answer her mother. It would be an ongoing battle to convince her mother otherwise. "He's shy. We're going to hit the mall and were wondering if Max could hang with you?"

Her mother bent and gave Max an awkward pat. "Does he have a cage?"

Max dropped to the floor, flattening his body against the Berber carpet and covered his head with both front paws and whimpered.

To be heard over the whining, she leaned forward. "Please, Mother, he just came from the pound. Putting him in a kennel would only traumatize him."

Nala wasn't sure if that was true, but he certainly acted that way. Her eyes narrowed as she looked at the quivering dog. He could very well be acting. His head and shoulders shook, but the rest of his body stayed solid.

Gwen knelt beside the dog. "I'm so sorry, sweetie-pie."

Nala managed to quell the urge to point out that Max didn't like baby talk, which was just as well because it would be hard to explain how she knew that. "Well, I see you two are getting on well. Remember to give him plenty of water."

Her mother looked up from her kneeling position. "Carbonated or still?"

"Tap water will be fine."

Max moved his paws to look up as if questioning her choice. If she allowed her mother to babysit too long, the dog would be spoiled. "I should be back in an hour or so."

Her mother waved her on. "No rush. I'm working on inventory. Besides, keeping Max will give me great practice for grandchildren."

That hardly seemed likely, but she wasn't going to touch that time bomb. A simple wave served as her escape. If she hurried, Max wouldn't be wearing a festive bandana and smelling of an expensive aftershave when she returned.

THE MALL DIRECTORY showed a box with a 201 on it for the maternity store. The second-floor escalator would get her there. Young mothers with strollers and others trying to herd children as opposed to pushing them crowded the wide aisles. An occasional pair of seniors in coordinated jogging suits would whip past her, more concerned about lapping everyone as opposed to looking in store windows.

On the second floor, she slowly scanned the area. As a teenager, she used to haunt the mall with all her friends. Mainly, they kept their haunting contained to the teen fashion shops, movie theater, and the pizza restaurant. No sign of the trendy store they shopped at. A candle shop sat in its place. Next to it was a cell phone store, then a lingerie store, and finally a store that announced with a big exclamation point, Preggers! Found it.

Models with angelic faces, rounded stomachs, excellent hair, and mysterious smiles wore the floral smocks. A chime sounded as she entered the store. A perky petite woman pranced out in platform shoes and a mini-skirt. "How's the new mother?"

Nala looked over her shoulder, expecting a pregnant woman, but no one was there. Obviously, the woman meant her. Her hand patted her belly, thinking it didn't feel all that rounded. If she had put on weight, her mother would have pointed it out. "Umm," she stalled, not wanting to pretend she was pregnant even though that was the whole purpose of the trip.

"I can always tell the brand-new mothers. You're probably still in the shock stage. The new ones always show up anxious to try out the clothes when their bellies are as flat as a pancake."

That made her feel a little better. "I heard you have some type of fake belly the women can use to see how they will look in the clothes."

"That we do. In fact, we have two. One is just a stuffed light-weight belly, but the other is the sympathy belly for the husbands. It's heavier and has liquid in it. Which one would you like to use?"

For her purposes, the lightweight one would work better, especially if she had to break into a run. "I think I'll go for the lightweight one. The floral dress on the model. Probably in a size 10."

That set the employee into motion as she hunted down the floral dress in the right size. Nala ducked into a dressing room that was filled with framed photos of happy babies and one small mirror that allowed her only to see the upper one fourth of her body. Could be that most women, while embracing the miracle of birth, didn't want to witness the vanishing waistline. Unfortunately, not being able to see her belly with the fake tummy attached didn't allow her to see if she made a believable pregnant woman.

A trio of knocks revealed Miss Perky, who opened the door and peeked in without waiting for permission to enter. Luckily, she was still dressed.

"Can I get you anything else?"

An idea made itself known. "Could I take the belly home to show to my boyfriend? I'll bring it back tomorrow. I'll buy the dress, too."

The woman looked unconvinced about the plan. Before she could tell her no, Nala added, "I'll buy two dresses. No, make that three." If her new detective persona was going to be a pregnant woman, she couldn't wear the same dress all the time. Even if men tended to look through expectant mothers, there was a chance they'd notice one who had on the same dress each time.

"Three dresses and you need to get the belly back to me before the evening shift. We get the most traffic then since most of the mothers to be have day jobs."

Nala agreed, hoping she could tail Gordon or Marvin as a bun in the oven chick. Max might have to be left home, which she was ninety-nine percent sure he wouldn't like. Even though many places were more pet friendly there were several places a dog couldn't go, but a woman could.

To save time, she decided not to change out of her dress and her trial belly. "Can I just wear this out?"

"YOU COULD, BUT you might want me to cut out the alarm tag first." She pulled a pair of scissors from her pocket and pointed to the collar of the dress.

"Oh, that must be what's sticking me in the neck." She unbuttoned the first three buttons of the dress and pulled the neckline out. After the woman removed the alarm tag and snapped off the price tag, Nala rebuttoned it.

Her intention was to grab two other dresses and be done. As she strolled past form fitting tube dresses and see-through lace outfits she wouldn't wear even when she wasn't pretending to be pregnant, she made it to the day dresses. The red and white striped one carried a two-hundred-plus tag. Who would pay that to look like a circus tent? After careful scrounging in the discount area, she came up with three dresses that cost her three hundred and fifty dollars.

She joked with the clerk as she rang up the dresses. "I can see why your business is in the evening. The women need day jobs to afford the clothing."

"They're career women." The clerk pushed out the information through closed teeth.

MISS PERKY MUST have stayed in the dressing room and sent out her grumpy twin to close the sale. "I'm sure they are."

"If you fail to bring the baby bump back on time, your card will be charged another three hundred dollars."

"What!" Maybe she heard wrong. "Did you say three hundred dollars?"

"I did." She gave a sniff. "Our bumps are imported from the United Kingdom."

"Do they fly first class?" The woman didn't even crack a smile. "Did I mention I work for the Bunco division of the police department that specializes in swindles and scams?"

Already she was working on perfecting her disguises. The Bunco thing was inspired, though most people though it was a game played by bored suburban housewives. The clerk did not recant the price, but merely raised an eyebrow.

"You should know my Uncle Elmer, then. He's a cop."

Oh, great, it was hard to know if the woman was telling the truth or bluffing her. "I'm sure my father knows him as a thirty-year-plus veteran and captain." Hopefully, the mention of her father would nail the blustering down.

Instead the woman held up the credit card and wrote something on a yellow sticky note.

"Hey, what are you doing?" Good heavens! Hopefully, she wasn't writing down her card number. That would be so illegal.

"Bonne. Wrote your name down so I could tell my uncle."

Great. She wasn't bluffing. At least, there was a Captain Bonne. She accepted the receipt and sack and promised to return tomorrow, then headed for the escalator. Who knew it would be so hard to pretend to be someone else? If Gordon was doing it, she wasn't sure how he kept from confusing his new self with his old one.

Reflecting on how much harder it was then she expected, Nala mentally calculated what to next do as the escalator carried her to the first floor. All she had to do now was to get to her car, grab Max, then do some reconnaissance work to determine which person to follow tonight.

Before she could leave the mall, she made a right turn in the direction of the pretzel vendor. As she waited for the hot pretzel, she considered the feasibility of giving Max a pretzel. If he were a person turned into a dog, she wouldn't have a problem with it. People ate all types of crappy food, while dogs ate…her nose crinkled. A pretzel would be okay.

"Nala!" a feminine voice called out.

There couldn't be too many people in the mall named after a

character in *The Lion King*. She turned to see who it was. Hurrying toward her was a classmate from her college English class. The recollection that her name started with an R presented itself along with her habit of eating sunflower seeds during class. Sometimes, she'd felt she sat by a large bird with all the seed cracking and spitting.

"HEY."

The woman gasped a little, and when she got her breath back, she spoke. "It's me, Robbie from British literature."

"Ah, yeah, I know. What's new?"

"Not much. No need to ask what's up with you."

Odd remark, but Robbie gestured to her dress. Nala stared down at the bump. "Oh." She should react and say something about the blessed event. Another memory pushed into her mind about Robbie. When she wasn't working her way through a mountain of sunflower seeds, the woman talked—a lot. "Great seeing you. I'm on my way to pick up Max, my dog."

"How nice. Saw the picture of you and Elvin on Facebook today. I envy you. You have a man who adores you, a dog, and a baby on the way."

"Things aren't always the way they look." She wanted to explain, but it would take longer than she truly wanted to take. Out of the corner of her eye, she recognized two of her mother's friends. Her best bet was to sprint for the exit before anyone else saw her. "Gotta run now."

The women she was hoping to avoid walked much faster than expected. Hiding would be her next best resort. A sidestep took her into a tobacco and pipe shop. An older woman looked up from where she was reading a magazine behind a counter. "I know smoking is an addiction, but, honey, you gotta stop for the baby."

Nala peered out the window, watching her mother's friends go by. No reason to give her mother's friends false information on the grandbaby front. Sometimes, she speculated that the father might not even matter if she presented her mother with a baby to spoil. Her father, of course, would feel differently.

Her hand went up, telling the woman she'd address her in a second. "Okay. I don't smoke. I was trying to avoid someone." She couldn't think of any reason for hiding out in the pipe shop, but surely everyone had someone they wanted not to interact with.

"Been there." The woman gave a raspy chuckle. "Are you done shopping?"

"Yes. Why?"

"I could let you out the back door, which opens up into the parking lot."

"You'd do that?"

"Sure. I remember how everyone and their sister wanted to give me advice on pregnancy. Everything from scary labor stories to reminding me not to mark the baby."

"Mark the baby?" The woman gestured to a beaded curtain that separated the public area from the storage room. "Forget about it. All that stuff is nonsense. This way." She held up the beads and allowed Nala to pass through before releasing them.

Unsteady towers of boxes created a narrow aisle to the door, which the helpful woman opened. As Nala passed through the opening, the woman commented, "As disguises go, yours needs work. At first, I thought you were pregnant until you walked across the store. You move too easily for a pregnant woman."

Chapter Ten

WHAT SHOULD HAVE been an easy disguise was quickly becoming a disaster. The clerk at the maternity store might say something about Captain Bonne's daughter being pregnant. If Robbie was the chatty type, which she was, there would be a good chance that Elvin would be labeled expectant father. The thought made Nala laugh. It certainly wouldn't work well with his *cool dude* persona.

Instead of dashing to her car to make a quick escape, she slowed her gait to try to approximate the speed of an expectant mother. The problem was she hadn't spent much time around mothers to be. Her friends opted for careers as opposed to families. Some were more like Karly and herself, who hadn't gotten the relationship part down. Things had to be different back in her parents' generation. They had an attitude that it was as easy to find a life companion as it was picking up a gallon of milk.

If only it were. She could count her former relationships on one hand, not using her thumb. None of them ended well. A few were like a fender bender where people grimace and exchange insurance numbers. It was the one that felt more like her future dying that made her reluctant to keep trying. After all, there were more singles than married folks, which had to demonstrate other people felt the same.

Inside the car, she hesitated, speculating on how showing up in a maternity dress would go over with her mother. A not-so-secret part of her mother would hope it was a message as opposed to being part of her job. The entire idea of posing as a pregnant female was not to attract attention. What she didn't count on was the reaction of those who knew her. Maybe the disguise would work better when she was an anonymous mother to be. Obviously wearing the disguise out wasn't her smartest idea.

Maybe Karly wouldn't mind her apartment serving as her personal changing room. Nala hurried to her friend's apartment and was ushered in on the first knock. Karly followed her into the bedroom.

"What's the deal with the photo of you and Elvin?"

"It's nothing. You know Elvin. He's a goof."

"True. He certainly looks happy in the photo, while you look surprised but still hot."

The yards of material made it hard getting the dress off, and the baby bump didn't help. "I'm not sure how pregnant women wear these dresses."

"Most don't. Haven't you noticed most get by with shorts and yoga pants as long as they can?"

"Nope." She pulled on her pants and perched on the bed to lever on her shoes. "I was told today that I didn't even walk like a pregnant woman."

"Show me." Karly gestured to the small stretch of carpet in between the bed and a dresser covered with dog figurines.

Nala pulled on her shirt and walked slowly across the floor.

"Yeah, you're no good at it. Your slow walk is what most teens do while looking at their cell phones. You need to keep in mind your center of gravity has shifted." Karly pushed out her stomach emphasizing the curve of her spine. "Every now and then, stop and put your hand on the small of your back. Don't wear high heels, either. No expectant mom does that more than once."

"It would be easier to run in athletic shoes."

"No mother-to-be runs unless she's being chased by a bear, except for those hard-core health nuts. You know, the ones who brag about how they ran the Boston Marathon while nine months pregnant as if they have something to prove to the rest of us."

As a PI, she didn't expect to be running, except for those occasions when she needed to be out of sight fast, which should only be a short sprint. She didn't have anything against runners in general, but Karly did.

Her toxic ex had been a marathon runner whom she met when he came to the shelter to find a dog to run with. He picked up both a black Lab and Karly. The two of them dated, if you could call being his support team while doing long runs as dating. After he ran the marathon and finished near the back, he dropped Karly and returned the Lab to the shelter. Personally, her friend acted more offended that he'd return the dog. Fortunately, Karly managed to place the dog with another runner. After that she never had anything good to say about running or runners.

"Running isn't my strong point, but plenty of pregnant women keep running. They even had belts and belly halters in the store for that type of thing."

"Yep. Ask yourself if you are going to be athletic pregnant or the run-of-the-mill pregnant?"

"The latter. Although, jogging with a running stroller with a doll strapped into it has potential, too."

"Until someone tries to look at the baby."

"There is that. Well, I should go get Max. I'm not sure if I should take Max with me?"

"Maybe not, especially if you don't know where your men are headed. I'm free tonight. I'd like to see how the dog is doing."

"Are you going to sense it or have an actual conversation?"

Karly stopped, resting her hand on the bedroom door. "He talked to you?"

"Talked. You make it sound like he said a word or two. The dog hasn't stopped talking. He keeps a running commentary on everything, except when someone else shows up, and then he shuts up. The other night he did say something when I was outside talking to Harry. I coughed and pretended it was me. My mother is convinced I have a secret boyfriend since Max is always so chatty in the background whenever she calls. I even let her think it since it's so much easier than explaining a talkative dog. If I did, she might have me kidnapped and taken to some mental health facility deep in the mountains with no cell service."

Her friend crinkled her nose. "I'm sure she wouldn't do anything that drastic. Besides, with Elvin posting your photo and you prancing through the mall in your pregnant attire, she'll have other things to think about. Tell me about Harry. Is he attractive? Is he under forty? Rich? Available?"

Karly had never met a man she didn't want to know the details on, unless he was a runner. It didn't do Karly a great deal of good since she'd never done much with the information, unless it was to match a man up with the perfect rescue pup.

"As for Harry, he has an office in my building. He appears to be under forty and is attractive in a geeky hipster way."

"What do you mean?"

Nala cocked her head to the side wondering how you could

explain someone giving out a geeky vibe. "I only saw him twice. The first time, he was carrying boxes. The second time was in the dark outside of the building. He's helpful, maybe too helpful in that kind of math nerd way."

Her friend lifted an eyebrow as she tapped her index finger against her cheek. "The geeky ones are the smart ones. Certainly, better than the man bimbos."

"Yeah, Karly, you've been through so many man bimbos." They both chuckled together. "I better head out now since I don't know when my guy will leave."

"Who are you following tonight?"

Her shoulders went up in a shrug. Discreet inquiries meant she didn't tell her best friend.

"Okay, be that way, but you'll tell me eventually."

"Honestly, Karly, do you tell me about every person who drops off a dog at the shelter?" Her friend smirked. Of course, she did, or at least the more colorful ones. "Bad comparison. Dog rescuer and private eye aren't the same thing."

"Whatever. Maybe you can hold out now, but we have wine and brownie night coming up."

"That's playing dirty." More than a year ago, Karly, Bethany, Simone, and Nala decided to make dates with each other to do fun things. At first, they would get all dolled up and go to places like dance clubs and the theater. It didn't take too long before they realized they'd rather veg in their sweatpants, watch videos, drink wine, and eat chocolate.

One night a week they did just that. Then it became one night a month, then Simone and Bethany dropped out. Bethany got married, which happened at the speed of light, while Simone always seemed to have better things to do, which translated as either on the hunt for a man or she already had one. Still, she could have spent one night a month with her friends.

"You managed to work the kennel guy flirtation out of me with macadamia nut blondies."

"Please, you were dying to tell me. Keep that thought. I need to go get Max before he wrecks Posh Interiors."

"See ya."

Nala used Max as an excuse since she didn't want to belabor the confidentiality concept. Freed of her cumbersome belly and dress that fluttered almost to her ankles, she managed the stairs to the parking lot at a breakneck speed. It was sad Karly couldn't get a house with a yard and be able to have a dog of her own. It might lead to her having several dogs and angry neighbors, too.

Maybe she pressed on the accelerator a little bit more than necessary, but in the sleuthing business you never knew when your target would be up and about. So far, she only had a tentative schedule for where Marvin should be and nothing definite on Gordon. As a CEO, he could come and go as he pleased. No need to be at work at a specific time or even stay the day. The only thing he had to do was show up for the board meetings and functions. Neither was happening this week.

Flashing lights showed in her rearview mirror. She pulled to the shoulder for what she assumed was an emergency vehicle or possibly a funeral. Oddly, the blue and white lights moved right behind her. *Dear, sweet Lord, say it wasn't so.* Nala flopped back in her seat.

Her father mentioned more than once how certain areas of the city were a speed trap with one road having a series of different speed limits. She knew this, but was too caught up on whom to tail first that she blew through the first slow-down section. Her mirror reflected the trim, uniformed figure approaching her car.

Didn't some women get out of a ticket by crying or showing some cleavage? That's what she'd heard, but she didn't know if the women who claimed such antics were truthful. Her eyes dropped to her T-shirt emblazoned with her old college name. Out of luck there, unless the officer was a fellow Butler graduate. Since she'd spent her formative years with her father, crying was so out of the picture.

"Ma'am, did you realize you were speeding?"

Her father always emphasized honesty and politeness with dealing with the law. "No. I was concentrating on work. If I'd been paying attention..." She turned to look at the officer. Her eyes climbed up the black-clad chest to his name tag, Goodnight. No, it couldn't be. Same face, same eyes, same lips that were working hard to remain firm if the quiver at the end was any indication.

"Understand. Could I have your license and registration?" He bent to peer into the car and blinked once.

"Is it possible you have a twin brother who is also a police officer?" she asked while handing over paperwork.

He took her license and registration, allowing their fingers to touch briefly. It shot a zing down her arm that she knew meant trouble even if Max wasn't along to tell her. He peered at the license, then bent to peer inside the car.

"Ah, I know what you're thinking." She didn't, but could hazard a guess.

"Do you, Ms. Bonne? And no, I don't have a twin brother."

"It might be something like..." She lowered her voice to what she considered a masculine timbre. "...oh, it's that charming woman minus her handsome dog."

He chuckled, which Nala decided was a good sign. No one had ever mentioned getting an officer to laugh might get her out of a ticket.

"It was more like it's Captain Bonne's daughter. This must be a test of some type. Well, at least she doesn't have the out-of-control dog with her."

"It's not a test. My father didn't send me. In fact," she beamed up at him the same way the first woman who tasted chocolate must have smiled, "it might be better if my father didn't hear about it. Since he taught me to drive, he takes all my little mishaps personally."

"Have there been a lot?"

"Enough. Whadya say?" Give her a wad of gum and she could be a gangster's mol.

"You really weren't going that fast, but you should pay more attention to the speed limit in the future."

"I will. I noticed you didn't run my registration." Maybe she should shut up before she got a ticket. "I have an honest face, right?"

"Ran it last night. Should have run it again, though. Who knows what havoc you've created in the last twenty-four hours?" He held up an index finger. "Don't tell your dad."

"I won't. Am I free to go?"

"You are. I'm confident I'll see you soon."

She smirked, realizing he meant he'd be pulling her over soon. "Don't be too confident."

Her eyes stayed on the rear-view mirror as he walked back to his car. Goodnight looked as good walking away as he did coming toward her. Not that it mattered. She knew better than most what it was like dating a cop. No way did she want to spend every important event alone.

At Posh Interiors, all the cars were gone except for her mother's expensive sedan. Gwen felt the right type of car conveyed the right image to her clients. Her father griped it was show-otty, which only confirmed her mother's intent.

The back door might be open. It shouldn't be if Gwen listened to her husband. Nala stopped, exited her car, and tried the door. Locked, which meant she had to use the buzzer. She pressed out a tune knowing it would both identify her and irritate her mother. At a youthful age, she'd discovered the doorbell could function as a musical instrument. Her mother was not a fan.

Gwen answered the door with a chagrinned-looking Max on her heels. It could have been the ornate gold and red bow tied around his neck that caused him to hang his head low. "Hello, sweetie. Max and I have had such fun together."

"I can tell."

"I think the bow makes a nice contrast against his coat. It really makes his eyes pop." She rested her a manicured hand on the dog.

"I bet it makes his eyes do something. Appreciate you watching him, but work calls."

Her mother grimaced at the mention of work.

Even though Nala knew, she'd regret asking, she did anyhow. "What is it?"

"Sweetheart, do you really have to go investigate Marvin? I thought it was a good thing to have Beverly come to you, but now I don't know."

"Why is that?"

"You're taking it all so serious. Pictures and everything. Even when a woman says she wants to know if her husband is cheating, she doesn't."

"What if it were Dad?"

Her eyebrows arched high as her hand flexed. "First, the man wouldn't be that stupid. If he was, I'd get the best PI and best divorce attorney his money could buy. Might even chip in some of my own money, too."

"So, why would your friend feel any different?"

"I just don't want to see her hurt."

"You're already judging the man. He could be taking scrapbooking lessons to make her a scrapbook."

Her mother snorted her opinion of the scrapbooking idea. "Still, it would be nice to know he wasn't shoving his shoes under anyone else's bed."

"Yeah, that's probably it. All this work could be little more than the man showing up at a weight loss meeting." That would involve it being held at the Masonic Lodge, which could happen.

"I hope so." Gwen handed her daughter a new leash complete with fake jewels. "Had Jaci run out and buy this for Max. No reason he can't glam up."

Her dog caught her eyes. *Please, get me out of here, now.*

Never mind explaining to her mother that Max was a dog, a male dog, and a working dog. He didn't glam up.

"Thanks. See ya." She clipped on the lead for her mother's benefit, although she could have sworn, he cringed.

As she walked out, her mother called after her, "Don't forget lunch on Sunday."

"I won't." Now that she was grown up and out of the home, they met every Sunday for lunch. It was ironic considering they seldom had meals together when she lived there with her mother and father's busy work schedules. Now, Gwen chose not to work on Sundays and her father's job didn't require him to. It seemed only natural to invite their daughter to their luncheons. Sadly, as the only daughter, she seldom had a better option.

Chapter Eleven

A TRIP HOME to drop Max off took longer than she expected. Max refused to go into the expensive kennel she'd purchased. A pitiful whimper had her leaving the dog free to roam the house. If she wasted any more time, she'd never catch up with any of her targets.

With any luck, she might be able to tail both men. Her schedule stated Marvin would be leaving work about now. Armed with a recent photo she pulled from Marvin and Beverly's social media site, she could be certain she tailed the right man. The slightly pixelated image looked about the same. Marvin hadn't gone for a trendy haircut, spray tan, or up-to-date clothing, which meant she had been following Marvin when Officer Goodnight had interrupted her the other night.

It wasn't long before the man in question wandered out of the building with a slight smile and headed to his sedan.

"All right, focus." Nala peered through her sunglasses, hoping the oversized oak tree shaded her distinctive car, making it difficult to identify. Once in the sedan, he carefully maneuvered around the cars, flipped on his turn signal to exit the parking lot, then slowly turned right. It wasn't the behavior of a man anxious to get to his secret squeeze. It did make it easy to follow him, though.

Marvin's habit of slowing for yellow lights allowed Nala to stay with him. All it would take was a glance into his rearview mirror to identify her. She glanced over to the empty passenger seat. "Wish Max was with me."

Max often had a pretty good take on mankind. If all else failed, maybe the dog could track people she failed to tail. Then again, maybe not. She suspected a good part of Max's tracking was mostly talk.

With Marvin's cautious driving, they hit almost every red light. Hadn't anyone told him if you kept at thirty-five, you could make it through all the lights? But then, that depended on the traffic not being too heavy. With the large IndyGo buses weaving in and out of the traffic, it slowed things down, not to mention the thousands of workers anxious to leave the city and reach their suburban homes with manicured yards complete with a basketball hoop in each driveway.

Once when Nala brought an exchange student home from college, she asked if all the basketball hoops attached to or near the houses were some type of altar. She laughed and told her it was to the great god of basketball, who was very popular in the Midwest and worshipped by many.

The sedan's right turn signal clicked on. Even with a compact car between her and Marvin, she was able to watch him turn onto the side street that led to the Masonic Lodge. What was up with the lodge?

This time she'd have to go in and find out what she could. The electronic sign out front announced private lessons available for piano, guitar, violin, art…well, she couldn't read the rest since she had to turn too. By the time she pulled into the lot, Marvin was out of his car and moving toward the door. She waited until he entered before dashing across the pavement where a child struggling with an instrument case caused her to swerve.

Inside the building, she saw Marvin's khaki-clad legs going up the stairs. She'd lost valuable seconds avoiding the youngster. A voice from behind her startled her.

"Can I help you?"

A weary-looking woman with hair so glossy red it could have come from a box of primary color crayons sat behind the desk. There was a small sign on her desk that read *Receptionist.* The romance book she held open in one hand demonstrated she did little more than question people as they came in. Maybe the regulars, like Marvin, weren't even questioned.

"Um…" She wanted to follow Marvin, and he was getting away. "I was trying to catch up with my father." Nala gestured to the stairs.

"Ah, Mr. Van Camp." The woman nodded, put her book down, and smiled. "Your mother is a lucky woman."

"She is?" Her voice swung up, demonstrating her surprise. Of course, she forgot for a second that for pretense purposes Beverly was her mother. "Oh, how?"

"Obviously, she's going to be a grandmother soon."

The disguise. She needed to stay in character. "Ah, yes." Her hand smoothed down the folds of her dress, trying to determine if her baby bump was crooked. "What other reason is she lucky?"

If she could get the information she needed from the talkative receptionist, this job would be closed in a hurry. Perhaps the fastest case in PI history.

The woman laughed and shook her index finger. "Ah, I bet your mother sent you to spy. Shame on her."

The woman had no clue how close she was. "Okay. She did, but don't tell Marvin. I mean Dad. Since I'm here, is there a ladies' room? I can't go thirty minutes or thirty feet without needing a bathroom."

"I understand, sweetie. There's one on the second floor. You have to go past the art gallery, and it's at the very end."

Nala waved as she headed toward the stairs, determined to walk slowly as befitted a woman in her condition. Halfway up the wooden stairs, she realized most expectant mothers would have asked for directions to the elevator. When she reached the second-floor landing, there were several people standing around in a lobby-like area. A few were seated and paging through magazines or staring at their cell phones. Most of them had an instrument case beside them. A few didn't.

To get to the other side, she'd have to work her way through the group. With her luck, a helpful individual might try to direct her to wherever she was going, which meant she needed to mention a class. A wall sign announced what class or event was on each floor.

The second floor was for private music lessons. She got that. There were also ballroom dancing lessons, yoga, and watercolors. Hard to imagine Marvin doing any of those. As far as she could tell he wasn't dressed for yoga unless he had on a leotard under his khakis. There could be a chance he had an artistic bone under his button-down shirt. Then again, this could be a cover to meet someone. If only she could just peek into the classes.

Her pace was unhurried as she read the notices on the door. A few were about upcoming classes and another warned against wearing street shoes on the dance floor. There was frosted glass on the window that didn't allow her to see inside, but she could hear voices. Marvin appeared on her right, but she couldn't determine which door he exited.

"Hey, Nala, what brings you here?" He gave her maternity attire a speculative glance, but didn't say anything.

"Oh, I thought I might take up watercolor painting." Her plan was if he were in painting class, he'd extol the virtues of it.

"Sounds good. Everyone needs a hobby, especially someone young like you. Otherwise, you'll end up like me, a man with no hobbies or trying to find something I could possibly learn at this late stage." The way he talked, you'd think the man was going to die in a matter of months. Marvin checked his watch then held up his hand. "Gotta go, don't want to be late to class. The teacher is a real drill sergeant."

Before Nala could reply, something bumped her knees. A boy probably around ten or more was wrestling with his oversized instrument.

"Sorry. This stupid bass fiddle is hard to carry."

"No problem," she assured the red-faced boy, then peered around for Marvin. Closed doors lined the hall with no sight of Marvin. He was definitely taking a class, but which one? Why would his wife mind if he took a class? Better yet, why hadn't he mentioned it? Peculiar.

It looked as if she'd missed her chance. Maybe if she hurried Gordon might be visible and tail-able. Although he didn't have a hard and fast schedule like Marvin, she did have a list of where he could be according to his secretary.

St. Elmo's Steakhouse, smack in the center of downtown, was a favorite haunt of his. Supposedly, he ate at the bar when he didn't have a reservation. She could try that, although it would mean wasting time finding a garage then walking to the restaurant. Why couldn't the man eat somewhere more convenient with its own parking lot?

Listen to her, complaining about everything. Well, at least as a pseudo pregnant lady, she'd take the elevator down with no guilt. She'd try the restaurant first and even get one of those spicy shrimp cocktails that were practically iconic as part of her cover. Her stomach made a rumble, probably seconding the idea. Maybe she could get some king crab mac and cheese if Gordon was there. It would appear odd if she breezed in and didn't eat.

The receptionist's desk was empty, which meant she struck out on getting any more info from her. The woman already demonstrated her pride in keeping a secret. No way Marvin would have confided an affair, but what could he be doing that would be worth telling a receptionist and swearing her to secrecy? Sometimes, the most improbable could be a possibility. Her lips twisted as she mulled over the possibilities as she exited the building.

Playing the bass might be a stretch, but that would involve an instrument. Inside the car, she sat for a second before a thought occurred to her. Nala slapped her forehead with the heel of her hand. "Duh. It's so obvious. He's taking dance lessons to surprise his wife." There was still the issue with Italian food, but that would resolve itself in some satisfactory way.

A twist of the radio dial and a punch to her favorite rock station sent upbeat lyrics soaring through her car. Instead of singing the regular lyrics, she sang out, "Marvin isn't a cheater!" He must be taking dance lessons for something special such as an anniversary, birthday, or an upcoming wedding.

Her first case was almost solved. The traffic gods were with her after she hit green light after green light. She even sneaked into the parking garage at after-hours prices. It was all good. She turned off the ignition, slammed the door, and headed for the street. There was light foot traffic as workers hurried home and couples strolled arm and arm to their evening destination.

The GPS on her phone told her to turn left, which she did. Thank goodness she had her phone. Her father enjoyed ribbing her about her poor sense of direction, especially when she called him when she got lost. A smartphone with GPS allowed her to be more independent. As long as she had cell service and a charge, nothing was stopping her from getting to her desired destination.

The navigation couldn't see everything, so she made a wide circle around the man panhandling but moved closer to the street musician playing the saxophone. Nala dropped a dollar into the music case before moving to the crosswalk.

St. Elmo's, while being popular, wasn't the biggest restaurant around. When the Super Bowl came to town, to keep patrons moving it was rumored they removed the chairs. She wasn't sure if that happened or it was just one of those things people repeat so many times everyone believes it's true. A regular urban legend like the hitchhiking girl in the prom dress.

The white walking man symbol flashed on, and Nala joined the rest of the people crossing. The lighted St. Elmo sign served as a beacon. Almost there and with any luck, Gordon would be, too. As she walked, her mind played with the idea that Gordon wasn't the billionaire businessman he claimed to be. A crazy thought, but Nala had had many such thoughts before. Her grandmother claimed the family had a strong history of magic attached to them. Perhaps that's why she ended up with a talking dog. Karly also knew she wouldn't have the heart to reject Max, knowing his history. She wouldn't put it past her friend to coach Max to get his history out there as fast as possible.

A line had formed in front of the restaurant. Not a huge line, just about six or eight people talking and milling about. If she just walked in, it might irritate, but even if she had reservations she'd still have to go inside and tell the maître d'. Nala acknowledged the people with a nod as she moved past them into the restaurant.

A waiter came up beside her as if herding her. "Can I help you?"

"No, I'm good. Just heading to the bar."

The look the man shot her was one shade less than total condemnation. He must assume she was an expectant mother with a drinking issue. She held up her hand as if to stop his false assumptions. "I'm going for the food, not the alcohol. Why take up a table if it's just me?"

The tight-lipped stare of disapproval lessened some, but didn't totally disappear. Geesh, wasn't the pregnancy belly supposed to make people ignore her? It wasn't working. Not only were they noticing her, but they were busy judging her lifestyle choices.

Her initial intent had to been to ask where the ladies room was and take a gander at everyone sitting in the bar area as she slowly strolled to the facilities. The waiter's disapproval sparked a rebellious streak that had her boosting herself up on a barstool.

When the bartender asked her what she wanted, instead of asking for an Elmo's Cola, the bourbon-infused soda, she requested water with a slice of lemon. Her head moved side to side as she attempted a subtle twist on her seat to check out the bar area. The lighting was subdued, but not absolutely dim as was so often the case in bars. Since the bar served as the entrance to the restaurant, a steady stream of people either arriving or leaving kept blocking her view.

A slight dip in one direction allowed her to see until someone blocked her view again. The bartender placed her water on the counter.

"Can I get you anything else?"

Oh, yeah, she'd have to order if she planned on staying to gawk.

Most restaurants didn't take well to people taking up a seat that could be taken by a paying customer.

"I'd like a shrimp cocktail and mac and cheese."

"Okay." The bartender paused, then added, "I guess you know the sauce is very spicy. Lots of horseradish. Some folks don't know."

"I've had it before. No worries."

Did he feel the need to warn her because of her pregnant disguise or did he consider her not one of the regulars? A few of the patrons wore suits, but most had on dress shirts while a few others wore jeans. The women's apparel varied from dresses to strategically ripped jeans. The jeans probably cost more than the dresses.

In her fashion summary, she picked out three men that resembled Gordon's vague description. One had on a Colts jersey. Nala dismissed him. It was hard for her to picture a CEO in a sports jersey outside of the stadium. Besides, when would he have had a chance to change from his business attire? It would be hard to take a CEO seriously who left the building looking more like he should be working in the mail room.

One of the other possible men had his head angled toward his date as if listening. There was no mention of Gordon being married, so he could date. Although, would a man take a woman to his own haunt or opt for something new? Nala never considered herself an expert on men, but she'd opt for somewhere else so as not to bump into friends who could skew the whole thing by saying something awkward such as calling her date by a former boyfriend's name.

Now would be a wonderful time to have some of those binocular glasses that would make her look prematurely old. Even a pen camera might be nice. A photo could be uploaded onto the Internet, and she could search for a match. All the free online programs depended on easily accessible databases to identify a person. That meant it couldn't access criminal records or even the BMV database, but people who have been in the news were usually locatable.

A waiter presented the bill, and the man handed over his credit card. Oh, no, they were leaving as opposed to arriving. She'd have to follow them and miss out on the food she'd ordered. Snickerdoodle, she was hungry too.

The man stood and helped his companion up. The woman stood about six inches taller than the man. Gordon was supposed to be very tall so it couldn't be him. Her shoulders relaxed as she watched the couple leave. The man placed a hand on the small of the woman's back. It definitely wasn't Gordon. Besides being too short, he showed a deep fondness for his date, which appeared totally out of character.

Her eyes went back to the guy in the jersey who was tossing back brews while joking with a couple of male friends. Would someone who avoided photos be the type to hang out with friends? Better yet, was he tall? The other guy had fooled her since he'd been sitting. One of the men motioned a waiter over and handed him his cell phone. The three friends mugged for the camera complete with throwing some type of hand sign.

No way would Gordon allow his photo to be taken, especially when it could be loaded to social media in a matter of seconds. Constance Bingham may have prejudiced her to the man, but as a professional she needed to keep a clear head. Honestly, she didn't rub elbows with CEOs. All she knew was they tended to make obscene salaries for doing practically nothing. When things went bad, they escaped with enough severance pay to buy a small Caribbean island.

Mr. Happy Beer Drinker wasn't Gordon. In her mind, the man would ask for a dry martini with top shelf vodka and three olives or something similar. There would be a slight sneer in his voice indicating that whatever they had wouldn't be good enough for his refined palate. That left the last man who was sitting alone staring at his cell phone and nursing a martini. Bingo.

Her shrimp cocktail arrived, causing her to smile at the server. Her first experience with the spicy sauce had her practically belching fire. This time she knew enough to shake off most of the sauce clinging to the oversized shrimp before popping it into her mouth. A mirror wall had various drinks listed but also allowed Nala to track the general movements of the people near the bar.

A man arrived in a dark suit with an expensive haircut and one shoulder a tad bulkier than the other. Obviously, he was carrying a weapon. If he went to all the trouble to get a primo haircut, he could have popped for a custom suit, too. Her eyes stayed on the mirror until she couldn't see him anymore.

Time to improvise. She fiddled with her purse hanging on the back of her bar stool and withdrew her cell phone. Gordon number three, the one with the martini glass, stood, and greeted Mr. Obviously Packing. They shook hands and then sat. Peculiar.

The man she assumed was Gordon was meeting some dude with a gun. Part of her wanted to jump to conclusions such as hit man or gangster, but wait, since this was Indiana, it could be almost anyone who convinced himself he needed to be armed at all times. The occasional sticker with a gun with a line through it indicating such areas were no-gun zones surprised her, probably because she never considered bringing a gun to the library, church, or the trampoline zone.

Until recently, she hadn't even carried one. Her father had her on the firing range before she even hit ten. He was a firm believer in women protecting themselves. When she started dating, instead of giving her a thoughtful talk her father insisted on defense techniques. On her first date, her father, after being introduced to her date, made a two-fingers gesture to his eyes, reminding her to gouge the eyes first, and another hand movement pointing below indicating she go for the nads second. The bookish fellow who intercepted the signals never asked her out again, probably afraid he'd be maimed on the second date.

She fiddled with her phone, trying to figure out how she could take a selfie and get Gordon and friend in the picture at the same time. The bartender arrived with her mac and cheese, which smelled like heaven.

"Hey, you want me to take your picture before you dig in?"

"Please." Nala tilted up the dish and smiled. She glanced over her shoulder and noticed she wasn't in a direct line to Gordon and friend. "Ah, wait, not, my best side." With a little effort, she managed to scoot the barstool six inches to the left.

The bartender held up the camera and thankfully didn't mention he was still shooting the same side. "All right?"

"Yeah. Go ahead."

Just before the shutter clicked, she ducked down. What would be the use of a photo with her big head in the way.

"Hey, you moved."

"Oops, I thought I had cocktail sauce on my face. Had to check. I'm good now."

"Do you want another shot? Since you weren't in the last one?"

As much as she wanted to say no, it would probably cause more speculation than she already had. "Sure." She made sure to turn her face slightly, exposing her mythical better side.

Truthfully, both sides were the same. As a teenager, she spent many angst-filled hours staring into the mirror, wishing she was beautiful or at least striking. Her father would affectionately tell her she was as cute as a button. So far, she hadn't come across any memorable buttons.

Her average face, which used to be the bane of her existence, could be useful now. She grinned for the photo and slipped the guy a tip for being so chill about the whole thing. Her eyes stayed on the mirrored glass as she dug into her delicious macaroni and cheese. The only time she'd see the men was if they stood up.

What she wouldn't give to hear what they were saying. A parabolic microphone would not only magnify Gordon and associate's conversation but everything else in the area. Ice cubes clinking in glasses would probably sound more like glaciers splintering. Then there would be the issue with hiding the oversized device. A purse certainly wouldn't do it.

She didn't have one yet, anyhow. Right now, she'd have to settle for shoe leather and her average, all-American girl appeal. *Oops,* they were moving. The bartender was at the far end of the bar. Nala waved, but failed to get his attention. A busty blonde painted into a tight red dress giggled at something he said.

Forget about it. The man would probably never turn and see her. She threw down two twenties, thinking if the man wanted a better tip than the five, she gave him for the selfie then he should have noticed when she was trying to wave him down.

She took one final mouthful of the King Crab Mac and Cheese and slipped off the stool to follow.

Chapter Twelve

A LIGHT RAIN fell, causing the streetlights to sparkle and a sheen to develop on the street. People hurried from one building canopy to the next while the prepared strolled down the middle of the sidewalk unconcerned with open umbrellas over their heads. Nala stood under the overhang for a few seconds swiveling her head in both directions, looking for Gordon and his friend. Nothing except for a sea of umbrellas and a covered horse-drawn carriage moving past, packed with tourists, which blocked her view.

She craned her neck and rocked up on her toes, but it didn't help. As soon as the horse and carriage passed, one of those mobile bicycle bars where people pedaled while drinking moved into her viewing range. Since the vehicle usually depended on the efforts of tipsy patrons it didn't move that fast. Her lips firmed as she realized Gordon had disappeared as if he were smoke, thanks to the attractions that made the downtown so popular.

People leaving the restaurant bumped her as they exited, re-minding her she couldn't stand there all day contemplating her next move. At least she had a trench coat in her car, which would suit considering the weather and her occupation. As she hurried to her car, she considered the issue with shadowing a target.

What she needed was an assistant or two. She could have texted one to warn them that Gordon was on his way out. The assistant could have trailed him. They'd meet up later at the office and discuss the case. There was also the matter of paying the person. Keeping things confidential, too. Yeah, the more people involved, the less chance of that happening.

The car garage loomed ahead. She hurried into the enclosure, glad to be out of the rain. Due to her father's lectures about parking garages being crime zones, she usually had her hand in her pocket with either her finger on the spray nozzle of her pepper spray can or two fingers poked through the cat eye keychain, with pointed ears to be used on an attacker, preferably their eyes. Even though her father insisted on training her in self-defense, she was the one who usually ended up getting hurt, like the time she pointed the pepper spray can the wrong way.

The cement staircase was eerily empty. Nala placed one foot on the first step and glanced back at the elevator. Normally, her father wasn't a fan of elevators, convinced a person could be trapped in one. Still, if there was no one there, who would trap her? Besides, it had to be better than dark stairs. As she turned to take the elevator, two well-dressed matrons appeared with shopping bags, which only confirmed her decision.

The women gossiped about shared friends as the elevator made its way up. The chatty shoppers only went up one flight, leaving Nala to travel the rest of the way by herself. As the doors closed, the elevator shuddered and gave a deep wheeze that made the lights flicker. *Great.* Out of the hundred and one things she worried about, dying in an elevator hadn't even made the list.

Her mind composed a scenario in the three-second interval when the elevator lingered between going up and dropping. Her father would lean over her dead, broken body murmuring about how she didn't listen to him when it came to elevators. A groaning metallic screech sounded before the elevator lurched into motion. A sigh escaped her lips as she tabled her gloomy scenario. Besides, it would have only been a one-story drop, not enough to kill.

When the doors finally opened, she leaped out, surprising a waiting couple. Instead of explaining, she strolled past the two without meeting their eyes, quelling her natural desire to apologize or explain. She had to. Such behavior, besides being a tad on the needy side, would just waste precious time and make her memorable.

Since it was a weeknight, most of the cars had left, probably headed home for an evening of fast food delivery and binge television show watching. Her baby blue beetle gleamed under the vapor light. She did love her car. When she received it on her sixteenth birthday, the car was already older than she was since it had come off the assembly line in 1980.

Their neighbor was obsessed with the distinctive cars and usually had two or three in his driveway in various states of restoration. Several times, Nala had gushed about them as they drove past. Apparently, her father had received the hint and presented her with one of the neighbor's recent rescues. She would have liked the bright yellow convertible with daisies, but that would have been too much of a risk for her safety-conscious father.

Even mentioning how much she liked the idea of a convertible resulted in stories of accidents he'd been called to involving them. Her lips had tipped up in a smile considering the absurd lengths her father went to for safety purposes and then urged her to follow him onto the force. It made no sense. Lost in trying to figure out her father's paradoxical behavior, she didn't register the upcoming car until she heard the tires squeal as they made a high-speed turn. Her head snapped up.

A large, expensive sedan hurtled her way. She stumbled back and sought cover behind a concrete pillar. Her heart raced as she glared at the fool who had almost run her down. The vehicle's tinted windows obscured the driver, but as he passed under the vapor light the silhouette of a man showed. The tiny observation window allowed her to see the general head shape, close-cropped hair, and sunglasses, which was weird considering the dimly lit garage.

Her heart raced as she leaned against the column. The cool concrete chilled her resting cheek, but she stayed in position, allowing her heart to slow and Mr. Crazy Driver to get far away from her. The driver was a menace and needed to be off the streets.

The sound of other people approaching pushed her into motion. She slid into her car she affectionately referred to as Sweetie and started the engine.

"Just be glad that crazy driver is gone." She pushed in the clutch and reversed. Her father was a big believer in people knowing how to drive a stick shift. His reasoning anchored in the belief that there would be no vehicle you couldn't drive. Sometimes she thought he imagined his life as an action hero movie, jumping from vehicle to vehicle, commandeering a taxi or a school bus, or even forced to pilot a plane. Never heard of it happening, but he always had contingency plans in place.

As a child, she had to endure Saturday morning escape sessions, where cartoon watching was interrupted by a klaxon horn that signaled, she had to crawl to her safe place to avoid the imaginary fire. The neighbors may have wondered what was going on, but if they knew her father, they could probably piece it together.

She exited the garage and headed to her office, which wasn't that far away. Her goal was to grab her laptop and load the photos she took. She'd used the facial recognition software available free online, but for this she might need to upgrade to something better. With Constance's generous check, she had the money to do so. The thought excited her so much she forgot to turn on the radio as she made her way down the street. Instead, she compiled a list of what she thought she might need for investigative purposes. There had to be some site online that detailed the more appropriate surveillance tools to use.

She caught the lights, made a few turns on red, and arrived at the office in record time. Maybe in the building's heyday traffic was much heavier, but that had to be a couple of decades ago. She had to park about a block and a half away again.

A light drizzle on the warmer asphalt created a mysterious effect, with patchy light fog on the ground. The occasional street light appeared like a star overhead. Nala struggled into her trench coat inside the car, determined to protect her costly dress. After all, it was a business expense.

Nala locked her car as she remembered the drunk that had accosted her when she parked here before. Her gun rested in her handbag, which she pulled her coat over. She patted the purse bulge as a slow scrutiny revealed no bodies stretched out in a drunken stupor. Most people sober or drunk had enough sense to get out of the rain. Her steps echoed on the empty street. Could have been the night, the fog, or even the rain, but something caused a chill to creep up her spine.

Her pace hurried as she rushed through the darkened areas where the lights were out. Someone needed to call and report the lights weren't working, and that somebody would be her. She glanced at the intersecting street sign and counted back to the dark lamppost. Third light from the corner. That's what she'd report.

Oof. Something bumped into her. A hand grabbed her shoulder. Nala instinctually dropped into a crouched position to avoid the grasping hands, interlaced her fingers and swung upward hard. Her intention was to hit his knees, but his cursing indicated her aim had been a bit off. He dropped to one knee and cursed even more before lurching into a standing position and awkwardly stumbling down the street.

"HEY, WHAT'S GOING on?"

She heard a man's voice and running feet. Please, don't let it be another thug. She jumped up, keeping her gaze on the retreating man as she slowly backed up, ready to make the run to her building.

The footsteps slowed as Harry from the office approached warily.

"You okay?"

She gestured toward the man moving down the street. Her attacker's swift retreat bolstered her sagging confidence. Maybe she did have what it took to be an investigator.

"Shook up, but I'll be fine." She inhaled and forced her shoulders back to convey confidence, which she did not feel at the moment. Her coat fluttered open, spotlighting her baby bump. Even though it was hard to be sure in the low light, she was almost sure Harry's mouth dropped open. "It's a disguise."

"Oh, yeah, I knew that." His obvious relief showed.

As they walked to the office, he took her arm as if she'd need help up the four-step entry. Nala wasn't sure if the baby bump inspired such behavior or her almost mugging. Normally, she would have pulled away, but his caring attitude felt right. It had been a long time since a man looked out for her, if she discounted her father. Sometimes she wished she had other siblings that he could spread his thwarted action hero persona protectiveness over.

They walked up the front office steps, and Harry used his keys to open the door. "I was getting ready to leave for the night when I saw you hammer that guy. You were magnificent."

"Thanks. Not sure I've ever been complimented on my defense techniques before."

"You should be, especially considering your chosen field."

"Yeah." She managed an ironic laugh at herself. "I thought it would be safer than being a cop."

"How so?" He pushed the door wide for her while giving her a confused glance.

It made perfect sense in her head. Honestly, she didn't want to go on the force as Captain Bonne's daughter. She would have to be better than the rest. Any advancement, honors, or awards she might receive would always be regarded with suspicion, as if she hadn't earned them on her own merit.

Their footsteps echoed as they marched up the interior stairs in tandem.

"Less of a target. You should know there are plenty of people who hate the police." Her shoulders went up in a shrug, realizing as she spoke that, as an excuse it had issues.

"Maybe. Still, most criminal types understand if you hurt or kill a cop, you bring the whole force down on you. Any judge will lock you away forever. What type of protection do you have?"

No use mentioning her Glock since she hadn't gotten it out. "Well, my father *is* a police captain. If anyone killed me, he'd make Liam Neeson in all those *Taken* movies look like a boy scout."

"Ha, explains why you're not on the force. Don't think I could work with my father, either."

Working with her father wasn't the issue, but it was kinda since she suspected he'd be all in her business.

Harry kept talking. "What your dad might do after your death is beside the point. The question is how can you protect yourself now?"

She lifted one eyebrow as her chin went up. What was it with men? No matter how harmless they might look, they always shifted into the alpha mode, which usually came with a mini-lecture afterward for the little woman.

One hand fisted on her hip as she considered what else he might say.

"Where's your scary dog?"

Well, that wasn't what she expected. After all that, he inquired about Max? "I had to leave him with a friend. The person I was tailing was in a restaurant."

"Yeah, restaurants are funny about not letting dogs in. Seriously, there are some people I wish they wouldn't let in and give the dogs a pass, at least some of them. Might be hard for me to take a little yappy dog yipping the entire time while trying to eat my sushi."

He liked sushi. Nala decided to file that tidbit away in interesting information she'd dispense later to Karly. No reason to mention the almost mugging. Her friend would fuss and tell her to reconsider her career option. She opened her door and gestured for Harry to precede her. Since he'd walked all the way up to the third floor, she felt obligated to invite him in. While he may not have exactly saved her, he possibly made the mugger think twice about having another go at her.

"Can I offer you some instant tea or coffee? My mom brought me one of those single cup machines. Might even have a sleeve of Girl Scout cookies left." She wasn't sure on that last bit, but she hadn't eaten them and there was no evidence of Max doing so. The one thing she could say is Max didn't eat plastic, paper, or the restaurant take-home containers. He just cleaned them out.

"You had me at Girl Scout cookies." He grinned, which made the skin around his eyes behind his tortoise shell glasses crinkle attractively.

"Ha. I better find them." She gestured to the boxes beside the orange couch. "Still working on getting organized." Her eyes dropped to his chest, taking a moment to check out his T-shirt. No TARDIS, but there was some sci-fi monster on it and a reference to a movie she knew she'd never seen. *Called it. Total geek.* Having correctly summed up her helpful neighbor didn't give her the fist-pumping triumph she usually felt. Turning way from Harry, she rooted through the box that held the flavored coffees. She held up the tiny cups to better read them. It wasn't easy making out the small print with just the overhead light. "I have glazed donut coffee."

"Seriously?" He grimaced a little, letting her know how he felt about the oversweet flavor.

"Ah, right, I'll look again." She pulled another one out and guessed by its butterscotch color that it probably wouldn't be a winner. "Hazelnut?"

"Nope. Don't you have any real coffee in there?" He moved closer as if he would take charge of the sorting through the beverage packs.

"My box. I'll do the looking." She pulled out a slender sleeve of cookies. "I did find these."

Harry plucked the sleeve out of her hand, tore it open, and popped one into this mouth. "The chocolate mint ones, my favorite."

"I thought you didn't like overly sweet things."

He offered her a cookie. "I didn't say that. I just want things to taste like what they are. That's why I want my coffee to be dark and rich. Cookies are supposed to be sweet." He picked another one out of the sleeve. "Like this, just the right amount of sweetness and chocolate."

"I hear ya." She held out a green cup. "Here's French Roast."

"That'll do." He reached for the cup and carried it over to the coffee dispenser, which he plugged in. He looked around for some cups, found one, and placed it under the spout before the liquid poured out. "Do you do this PI stuff all on your own?"

"So far, but after tonight I decided another person would be handy."

"Because of your almost mugging?"

"No, not that. I blame myself for not being more observant of my environment. I know better. Another pair of eyes would have come in handy when the man I was following left the restaurant. Someone outside could have at least noticed which way he went. By the time I left money for the bill and got out the door, there was no sign of him. It was like he vanished."

"Hmmm." His hand went up and smoothed his beard. "You didn't see anything?"

"Oh, you mean besides a white carriage full of tourists or what I assume were locals pedaling one of those bicycle bars around? Nada. Nothing."

"Sounds more like he grabbed a cab. He probably called one from inside. He left when it came. Simple as that."

Nala snatched the sleeve of cookies from Harry and bit into one. *Taxi.* Why hadn't she thought of that? Someone outside would have spotted that. "Yeah, that's a possibility. Maybe I could get Max to watch the outside for me."

Harry laughed. "Yeah, like your dog could report back or something."

"Something like that." She assumed Max would stay where she told him, especially if he knew it was work.

"You must have a real talking dog. That or you're a pet psychic." He waggled his eyebrows. "Which is it?"

Neither one sounded all that great. "My odd suggestion must be the shock talking." Her shoulders lifted in a chagrined shrug. Her laptop case rested against the couch leg. She bent to grab it as she responded to Harry. "I got what I came for. Now, I need to go take care of my pet. I appreciate you walking me up to my office."

"Ah." He held up his cup. "I detect the bum's rush. May I ask what set you off?"

"Nothing." Her shoulders went up in a shrug. "Just been a long day, that's all. Maybe I'll see you tomorrow."

"Possibly. I'll walk you to your car."

Even though the idea of returning to the place she'd been attacked didn't appeal, asking Harry to walk her to her car might indicate a connection that wasn't there. He might take it wrong or, worse, she might. Then everything would be weird.

They ended up walking out together. Harry's car was directly past hers on the same side. When she flipped on the headlights, they spotlighted a sticker on his bumper. *Using your turn signal is not giving information to the enemy.* Hard to know if the declaration would be considered geeky or not, but it made him intriguing. A long sigh filled her car. Right now, since her life was in transition, she didn't need intriguing.

Chapter Thirteen

L AST NIGHT ENDED with a happy Max wolfing down the pretzel she'd bought him at the mall while Nala planned her tailing activity. It was a new day and she was back in the car keeping a discreet distance from her quarry. She had to leave Max back at the house since she wasn't sure where she might be going.

Her lips twisted as she debated telling Beverly her husband wasn't cheating since she was almost sure of it. Whatever Marvin was up to had her baffled. She'd followed a man who was terrified of flying practically to the airport before he turned off at a small office building, practically perched on the tarmac. Instead of a business sign announcing what it was, it only had a large street number outside, probably for those who were looking for the building.

Her vigil on the place was short lived. She watched a half dozen people come out dressed in business attire, get into separate cars and leave. The shift must have finished for the day. A security person approached her car. Nala abandoned the idea of dashing off, sure her license plate would be made and put out as an all-points bulletin. Security professionals tended to view people loitering around airports as suspicious.

She might as well pretend to be a confused female. Unfortunately, male cops tended to accept the bimbo routine without question, making her wonder how many actual criminals had done as much. As the older man with a crew cut approached her car, she rolled down her window.

"Hello, officer. I'm here to pick up a friend, but I know I'm not supposed to wait in front of the terminal."

"True." He gave her a casual once-over but didn't ask for proof of ID. "You know there is a cell phone lot where you can wait."

"Really?" Her eyebrows went up to express astonishment, which she hoped wasn't overacting. "Since when?"

The officer's brow furrowed, and his eyes rolled up. "Ever since the airport opened in 2008. I'm pretty sure the old terminal had a cell lot, too, but I didn't get hired on until 2011."

"Where is it?"

"You have to drive past the terminal, and it's off to the right. Once your friend calls, you'll have to circle around to pick her up."

"Will do." She beamed up at the officer as if he'd given her the winning lottery numbers. "I'll head over there."

Nala waited until the officer walked back to his sedan before starting her car. Now, she'd have to go to the cell lot and hang out there for ten minutes or so before leaving. It should be long enough to lose herself in the various vehicles coming and going. Unfortunately, Marvin would leave without her seeing. If she tried to nose her way back over, it would probably result in an airport lockdown.

Too bad she chose not to bring Max with her. She could have opened his door with instructions for him to escape into the unidentified building. Her only option would be to follow him. Tomorrow, she'd try that with a different car.

GOOD CHANCE THOUGH that whatever the building was would be closed on Sunday. Then there was the issue of another car. She'd have to borrow one with a semi-believable excuse. Since she would be at her parents' house for lunch on Sunday, maybe her father would let her use his ancient pickup. The reason she'd give would be she had to move something. Nothing too heavy or he would insist on helping. He'd probably insist on helping anyhow.

Her phone chimed as she grimaced, trying to figure out a story. In her entire life, she'd never put one over on her father. Not only was the man excellent at his job, but he also had the nose of a bloodhound. He'd sniffed out when she tried her first cigarette and her first drink, although not at the same time. Back when she was sixteen and wanted to go out with a local bad boy, she told her mother she was staying overnight at Karly's. No way could she have floated that fib past her father.

LATER, HER FATHER showed up in uniform at the local pizzeria where she and her date were and invited himself to their booth for a friendly talk. After the talk, which included relating the various run-ins with the law her date had had, Nala ended up going home in the squad car. Instead of being grounded for life, her father mentioned how disappointed he was in her, which had bothered her much more.

Another chime from her phone stopped her stroll down memory lane.

Her finger swiped to the right, and she held the phone to her ear, thinking how weird it would be if it was her father calling.

"Hello."

"I've got it," Karly enthused from the other end.

"Got what?" Nala was almost afraid to ask, but normally such a declaration involved a dog that would be perfect for her. Since she already had a dog, it couldn't be that. The white security car slowed as it passed the cell lot. The crew-cut hair of the driver indicated it was her officer from earlier. He might even be checking to see if she even went into the lot. If so, he was more thorough than some.

"A spell book. We can fix Max so he doesn't talk anymore."

The idea of making Max mute, except for the occasional bark, felt wrong. It would be the same as taking a carving knife and extracting his personality. A talking, often wise-cracking canine was who Max was. Besides, if he couldn't talk, how would he help her with her cases?

Karly spoke directly into her ear, shattering her moment of reflection.

"Are you still there?"

"Ah, yes, I am, but we don't want to rush into anything. We're not witches." She hoped that would be the end of the conversation.

"Speak for yourself. You know good and well that I always wanted to do magic."

"Yeah, I remember when you wrote that girl's name that you hated three times and burned it in hopes something bad would happen to her. Whatever happened to her?"

There was silence, making Nala wonder if the call had dropped. Finally, Karly answered in a sheepish tone.

"She won some type of full-ride scholarship, married a wealthy doctor, and moved to California."

"Hmmm, and what was that spell supposed to do again?"

"Stop it, Nala. You know what it was for. Maybe it was a delayed-reaction spell, and it just hasn't taken effect yet."

Karly, for all her blustery talk, didn't have an evil bone in her body, which made her a good match for the shelter. "I'm betting you didn't want anything truly bad to happen to her. It's all about intention."

Her friend grunted, allowing Nala to elaborate. "Sometimes things seem so incredibly important, but later, in hindsight, not so much. Several times I concocted revenge scenarios in my head involving Jeff. Usually, I'd look gorgeous when he was out with his male buds, and I'd shimmy past the table only to have his friends inquire who the hot babe was. In the end, I realized I no longer wanted to make the effort."

Karly cleared her throat, forcing Nala to pull the phone away from her ear. "Please, do you have to do that into the phone?"

"Sorry. Do you want Max to keep talking?"

"It's not so bad."

"If you say so. Before you picked him up from the pound, he made a teasing comment when the bottled water man bent over to deliver the water. The water guy thought I made it."

"It's true he doesn't quite have all the social niceties down, but who does?"

"Look, you're defending him. How sweet."

"Okay, I'll say it." Her nose crinkled a little bit, knowing what her friend wanted to hear. "You were right. You made a pet match."

"Cue the music. I'm good!" she announced with her normal cheeriness. "Just think if I could do this with humans, people would pay me big money."

A blue compact exited, leaving the very recognizable vintage Beetle as the only car in the cell lot. She'd have to go now to keep from being recognized. Too long in the lot and she'd be considered a suspicious lurker. "Gotta go. Talk to you later."

No way would she talk on the phone, drive, and not be spotted. With her luck, some eagle-eyed acquaintance of her father would mention it in passing. Technically, talking on the cell phone wasn't illegal, although using a hands-free phone was preferred. Texting while driving was a ticketable offense. Holding a cell phone could be confused with texting, although she could tell the police to check out those who were intently staring at their laps if they wanted to catch offenders.

Traffic increased on the 465 Loop as she headed east to her home. Max would be waiting for her, possibly staring at the door, bemoaning her absence. The thought had her grinning as she imagined his welcome. First, he'd give several delighted barks, spin in a circle before placing his front paws on her shoulders and giving her face a swipe with his tongue. Yeah, she could handle being a dog companion. Karly had insisted she not to use the word *owner* because it sounded too much like slavery.

Maybe she should ask Max if he minded the word. Orange barrels and road construction flashing lights reminded her to proceed with caution.

Too bad no one told the jerk behind her, who disliked her slowing down and swerved around her only to cut in front of her, mauling an orange barrel in the process. The barrel wedged under the SUV, forcing the inconsiderate driver to pull to the shoulder. Nala forced herself not to smile as she passed, but it didn't stop her from mentally rejoicing. Karma seldom worked that fast, but it was satisfying when it did.

Two stoplights and three right-hand turns brought her to a quiet subdivision of modest ranch homes with carefully groomed yards. A few of the residents were outside watering their flowers or sweeping their sidewalks. The small house she rented suited her needs and surprisingly allowed animals since her landlady was a pet owner.

The curtain sheers moved as she bumped into the driveway. Ah, her pup was waiting for her. It made her a trifle sad that she hadn't stopped for a treat. Maybe they could go back out later for a snack after she ran the image from the other night through her facial recognition software. She should have done it last night, but she ended up staying too late at Karly's, discussing Harry's date worthiness and the unfairness of men eating whatever they wanted and never gaining weight. Although, she had a theory on the last one. Men only pretended to eat whatever they wanted when they were around women.

Once she turned off the ignition, she grabbed her purse, ready to greet her newest family member. Should she sneak in and test his guard dog ability? Probably not since she'd seen the curtains move, proving he knew of her arrival. Voices came from her house. One was a woman's voice. *Who was in her house?* Were they trying to steal Max? Oh no, they were trying to steal her unique dog!

Her grip tightened on her keys as she slid the other hand into her purse and pulled out her weapon. The only time she'd fired it was at the shooting range. Hopefully, she wouldn't have to shoot. Perhaps the sight of an angry pet companion wielding a gun would do the trick. Although the term pet companion didn't drum up any images of kick-butt action heroines.

She slipped the key into the door and very carefully opened it about an inch, then kicked it open. "Ah-ha! I caught you in the act."

Max tumbled off the sofa, scattering slices of bread across the living room floor. The television was on and turned to the soap opera channel, which explained the woman's voice. A red-faced actress was accusing the other woman of something, but Max was the guilty-looking one.

He hunkered down, his muzzle on the floor, his ears half bent forward, and his eyes stared up at her. "I was hungry." He uttered the words in a plaintive plea.

"I left your dog food dish filled."

"Yeah, I appreciate that. Ate the food and I was still hungry. There was a loaf of that spongy bread that often has meat on it. Hate to tell you this, but you got a bad loaf. No meat. Checked every slice."

Nala suspected Max was playing her and she should scold him, but his eyes just about melted her heart. Maybe she should have bought a larger dog dish. Tomorrow, if she had to leave him, she'd make sure to leave plenty of food. "What's the deal with the television?"

"I laid on the remote and it came on. Not having thumbs prevented me from changing the channels. I'm more of an *Animal Planet* kind of guy, but I'm starting to get into this show. You see Serena, the screaming one, isn't as mean as she seems. There's been a great deal of disappointment in her life. The man she loves turns out to be her twin brother. They were separated at birth."

Nala held up her hand. "Say no more. I'm already invested in *The Bold and the Ruthless*, I don't need another show. Besides, I need to fix supper. Something that doesn't involve bread."

Max made an audible gulp that made her wonder. A half-chewed empty container of yogurt lay across the edge strip separating the kitchen floor and the living room carpet. Then there were the shredded paper towels she used to soak up the bacon grease. The junk mail she threw away yesterday decorated her linoleum along with a perforated Styrofoam takeout tray.

"Max! You got into the trash and flung it all over the kitchen!"

The German shepherd slipped around the corner into the kitchen, keeping his head down. "I said I was hungry. Nothing in your storage unit tasted that good. Sorry, if you were saving it for dinner."

"It wasn't to eat!"

"I have to agree with you on that. Smelled good, but nothing tasted even close to how it smelled."

"It was garbage." Nala sighed heavily and placed the junk mail back into the trash can. "I suspect you may have been let go due to issues besides talking."

"No need to be ugly. I'll help." He picked up the Styrofoam tray and deposited in the trash can.

The small action proved that at least his heart was in the right place, even if his manners were non-existent. "I think you need to learn some basic ground rules."

"This wouldn't have happened if you took me with you." His ears perked up, and his eyes looked hopeful.

Suspicion took shape as she considered the scene when she entered. Nothing that bad had happened. A loaf of bread bit the dust, but that loaf was probably already stale. There was some trash on the floor. Considering she'd seen dogs with shaming signs next to destroyed drywall, unstuffed couches, and chewed-up designer boots, what Max did was mild in comparison. It could almost have been a set-up that would lead to him suggesting he should ride along for safety purposes, but that would require some logical thinking. Even if he could talk like a human, he couldn't think like one. Or could he?

"Remember Officer Goodnight?" Nala sure did. It was hard to forget a man who filled out a uniform the way he did. Growing up surrounded by black uniforms, she tended to give them the respect they deserved. Just maybe that made her give a cop another look knowing what went into the job, but that didn't make her one of those groupies that went all liquid at the sight of a crisp uniform and a badge.

Max cocked his head as if thinking, "Who?"

Seriously, the dog somehow forgot probably the most embarrassing incident in her life. "You know. The cop. The one who stopped me outside the Masonic Lodge where you played keep away with the—never mind." Her face flushed even talking about the event. If she kept to all the traffic rules, she'd never have to worry about encountering the man again, which would be just as well since he probably thought she was nuts.

"Oh him." Max nodded his head. "The one who wanted to…"

"No." She held her hand up. "No need to elaborate."

"Humans," he managed a dismissive sniff, "can be so weird about a natural function. Then, on the other hand, you can be so quick to deprive us dogs of the same drive."

The dogs didn't leave the shelter until they were fixed to decrease the number of unwanted puppies. "I had nothing to do with that."

"Yeah, I know. Just pointing it out."

"I noticed. As far as taking you with me, sometimes I just can't because I'll need to enter buildings where dogs aren't allowed and you know if I left you in the car—"

Max finished the sentence for her. "Someone would try to break me out or report you to animal control. I know, but what if you kept the windows down, and if someone tried to rescue me, I'd simply tell them I was on the job."

Her fingers gripped the paper towel and tossed it into the trash can for the second time. "Yeah, you could do that, and it sounds good in theory. Most things that sound workable seldom are. It could cause someone to go into cardiac arrest. Might have someone think you're possessed and try to exorcise you."

"Been there, done that." Max gave a full-body shudder. "There has to be some way."

"You'd think, especially with people showing up with their dogs everywhere. Tell you what, I'll take you to my parents' house for Sunday dinner. This will be your chance to impress me with your excellent manners." If she took Max, it would give her parents something else to talk about besides her career change or love life.

"I can do that. What's your mother serving? I'm partial to steak." His lips softened into a blissful expression.

"I bet you are. However," Nala stood, picked up the trash can and placed it on the counter to avoid a repeat performance. "Dinner will be for the people. Since Mother has decided that my father's health needs a boost, we'll be eating something wild caught or free range. More likely it will be some type of sprouts, beans, and an ugly fruit that I've never heard of, but is chock full of vitamins. Even if my mother decided to make you a plate, you wouldn't like it."

His ears drooped a bit. "Maybe they might bring something in, like ribs."

"Dream on. That would only happen if there was someone there other than family, in particular, a man. My father has very firm ideas of what consists of male food, which could possibly be whatever you might like to eat, including steaks, ribs, chicken wings, and nachos."

A small canine whimper sounded as she named each food item until she got to nachos.

"Don't care for nachos. It's not very filling and very little meat, rather like the kibble you left me."

Nala rolled her eyes as she washed her hands, twisted off the water faucets, and leaned against the counter. "I suppose you'd like a hamburger for dinner."

He gave an excited bark. "Now, you're talking. Cheeseburger. Make that two."

It would be a mistake fixing a burger for a dog, but she did it anyhow. Maybe there was some better dog food out there that Max would like. Probably not as much as a burger, though. The rest of the night flew by as she uploaded the picture into the facial recognition program, ran it on Gordon, and got nada, nothing. She expected as much, which just showed that the man worked hard not to be photographed, which was weird.

Gordon had the looks of a Viking warrior garbed in a Brooks Brothers suit. People might call women vain, but in her experience, men could be just as vain or more so. You'd think every time a camera was around, he'd be in front of it. Then, there was the second thing. Free facial software was worth exactly what she paid for it.

The picture she took at St. Elmo's filled her screen. Even though Gordon's mouth was open as he talked with his table guest, his head was slightly turned, looking in the direction of the bar, the bartender, and her. His eyes were brown not unlike Max's. Using the zoom feature, she enlarged his head to almost life size. The dead eyes staring back at her reminded her of a zombie or a cyborg. Creepy.

Maybe she'd get a better result from Gordon's companion. The loading wheel spun for what she thought was eons until an image finally materialized. An Iowa newspaper article that detailed a triple homicide of a family featured a photo of the man with the expensive haircut she'd spotted inside St. Elmo's. Yeah, same guy in a prison jumpsuit. She would bet on it. So, why wasn't he in prison? A better question would be why was he in Indianapolis talking to a man with dead eyes? Whatever it was, it couldn't be good.

Chapter Fourteen

NALA'S HOUSE FACED west, which meant the morning sunlight didn't stream through the windows. She snuggled back down under her covers once she realized that she didn't need to go to school, and it was Sunday. She might have to work late as a private eye, but so far for the three days she'd been working, there had been no early morning duties. The exact opposite of preschool where she had to be in the classroom before seven, laying out the materials for the day. If there was a need to copy anything, she'd have to be there about thirty minutes earlier. Inevitably, the copier would be jammed, or it would need toner, and the school secretary wouldn't have arrived. No one else had a key to the supply closet, and everyone knew that the teachers were just itching to sell laminating spools on the black market.

Ah, Heaven. Nothing to do, unless she counted lunch with her family. Maybe she should shadow both Marvin and Gordon, although Marvin would probably spend the day at home. Gordon was a different case. What she needed was a tracking device affixed to his car. At least it would give her a general idea where the man went. Using a GPS to track him might be illegal. She'd deal with that later. Right now, she'd like to get back to her dream about the sexy guy with the lovely accent named Orlando who was brushing her hair on a tropical beach. Such a lovely dream. It had everything, except unicorns and butterflies.

Eyes shut, she took a deep breath, trying to visualize the beach and her foreign man candy. *The waves were frothing at their bare feet while a seagull circled overhead sounding his raucous call. Orlando smoothed the hair away from her face and spoke.*

"Are you going to sleep all day or what? People think dogs sleep all day, but personally I'd put you up against any canine."

Max. Grabbing her pillow, she held it around her head as she rolled away from the dream destroyer. No hope of getting back to sleep now. The bed groaned as Max jumped on it. His paws stepped around her, but one landed right on her stomach. *Oof!*

"You did that on purpose."

"No, I didn't." Max pushed his wet nose into her ear. "That was on purpose. See the difference?"

"Stop. Yuck!" She swatted at his legs, trying to push him away. "You're like the annoying little brother I never had. Hard to believe I begged my parents for one. Please, leave me alone."

"I'd like to, especially since you're such a grouch in the morning, but I gotta go."

"Go where? It's Sunday."

"Outside. My outdoor urinal, unless you're not that picky about where I go."

The possibility that the large dog might initiate her comforter or, worse, her mattress, had Nala rolling out of bed and sprinting for the back door. Max followed her with an uplifted head and a bounce in his step. When he reached the open door, she would have sworn he winked.

Was she up to hosting a canine with a wide streak of smart aleck? It might be the equivalent of having a twelve-year-old male cousin complete with fart jokes, only in Max's case it was poop commentaries. There could be worse things.

Her closest neighbor had six tiny yappy dogs that all barreled into their yard and barked their discontent at the new dog in the neighborhood. Max pretended not to notice the little fuzzballs and walked regally back into the house.

"What were they saying?"

"Look, it's a real dog. It's easy to believe the species descended from wolves when you see such a magnificent creature."

Nala laughed. "I'm so sure they didn't say that." Max had a sense of humor, which surprised her despite Karly insisting that all dogs had personalities. Some were healers, others pranksters, and there was always more than one free spirit in the shelter.

"Something similar."

"Ha, I've lived next to those dogs for two years. The six of them probably had to bark in sequence to make full words."

"Okay, person who-knows-all-about-dog-speak, what did they say?"

"Dog. Big Dog. Hope he doesn't eat us."

Max gave her a long look, then shook his head. "You're spot on. Maybe you do speak dog, at least yappy dog."

Wow! She'd never given it a thought before, but there were several types of non-verbal communication she'd picked up on, including the guilty look most of her former students sported at one time or the other. Her job was to figure out the incidents they'd created. Sure, it was easy if they still had the permanent marker or the scissors in their hand. It might have been that skill along with her early observation training by her father that made her consider a job as an investigator. More likely, it was the fact she knew who the culprit was ten minutes into the televised mystery show.

There could be the fact that television writers weren't trying to be too secretive, hoping to get the viewer rooting for the detective to unravel the clues as fast as possible. So far, the only thing she figured out was the seemingly innocent people, such as Marvin, still appeared to be so while Gordon oozed suspicion. But so far, she couldn't pin anything on him besides hanging out with bad company. The people who hadn't done that she could count on one hand.

Max nudged her leg. "Thought we were going to your parents for lunch after breakfast."

"Food, food, that's all you ever think about." She smiled as she said it. It was nice for a change to have someone around the house to talk to. Since she moved into the darling rental her parents had located for her in a safe neighborhood close to both a police and fire station, she'd never had a meaningful relationship serious enough for a man to hang out at the house and discuss the trivial details of the day.

As she picked up the bag of kibble, her forehead furrowed, trying to remember if she'd even had a boyfriend with a sense of humor. Nope, not unless she counted Ronny back in high school. His claim to fame was balancing a bucket of flour on a half-open classroom door so when their math teacher entered, he was doused with powder.

The quiet-spoken geometry teacher waited until the laughter died down, cleaned his glasses, sent Ronny to the office, and went on with his lesson. Come to think of it, Ronny wasn't funny, just a mean-spirited practical joker who got his jollies off making other people look silly. It only took a handful of dates for her shallow high school self to pick up on that.

Dog nails clattered against the counter as Max jumped up to see what she was doing. "Not that again. How about some eggs?"

"I told you I'd buy you something better when we're out. We don't have eggs. Besides, all I'm having is toast. It's important I eat heartily at my parents or my mother would think I'm anorexic. It's weird. Now that I'm adult and Mom has more leisure time with her employees helping to run Posh Interiors, she has plenty of time to focus on me."

"This is a terrible thing? I like attention."

"Don't I know it. I suppose it isn't, but I guess I'm at the point that I'd like to run my own life with no input from my parents."

"Hmmm." Max managed a sage nod and added, "So why are we going over there again?"

"It's kind of a tradition. Now, if something important came up like a vacation or something, they'd understand my absence. Besides, we don't spend much time on the phone catching up. Sunday lunch is about it."

"You do realize you're justifying things to a dog."

"Yeah, thanks, Max. What do I owe you for your counseling expertise?"

"Toast with peanut butter would do it."

"Of course, but don't think I'm doing this every day. You need a balanced diet."

His large eyes watched her hands as she withdrew the jar of peanut butter from an upper cabinet. Her hand stopped in mid-air, holding the jar. "Wait, we don't have any bread. Someone we both know destroyed the loaf."

His front paws slipped off the counter, backed up a few steps, and hung his head. "My bad. Guess it's dry, tasteless dog food for me."

"You got it. The real question is what will I eat?"

An hour later, after swilling down a soda and gobbling an energy bar, a meal she had previously warned the pre-school students' parents that no good would come of, she stepped into the shower. Normally, she didn't make a production of dressing up for her parents. The couple times she did primp, they both teased her about going on a date afterward. One time she actually had a date with an actuary from an insurance firm she'd met on an online dating site.

While drying her hair, the memories of the humorless man and painful date came back. She'd used her best jokes, even kidded him about being a bean counter, but all he gave her was the same blank stare.

Her hair was probably as good as it was going to get. She shut off the hairdryer and stared into the mirror. A cute face stared back at her with its pert nose and a smattering of freckles. Yeah, she'd never be a sex symbol. Never Barbie, always Skipper. A swipe of mascara on her upswept lashes and some clear lip gloss completed her makeup.

Max pushed the bathroom door open, demonstrating his lack of boundaries or possible impatience. "Hey, Max, since you so rudely shoved your way into the bathroom, I have a question for you."

"Shoot."

"Why do you think some men have a sense of humor and others don't?"

He cocked his head one way, then the other. "Explain sense of humor."

Right, some expressions he might be unfamiliar with. "Well, ah." When it came right down to it, sense of humor wasn't the easiest thing to explain. It was simpler to determine when someone had one or didn't. "It's the ability to laugh at your mistakes instead of getting mad, even able to joke about them later. Sometimes it can be something as simple as a word pun."

"Confidence."

"That's it."

"Yep."

Her reflection wrinkled its nose as she contemplated the simple answer. "Confidence. Makes sense in a way. The confident person doesn't overthink a mistake or worry if he'll be judged on one little stumble."

"Yeah." Max agreed, nodding vigorously. "Let's head out to your parents' for lunch." He emphasized the last bit with a bark. "Do you think your dad will like me?"

If she didn't know better, Nala would have thought Max sounded anxious. "You already met him at the fire."

"Yeah, but it was dark."

"He remarked on what a handsome dog you were."

"Excellent eyesight, but this time will be the real deal."

Nala skirted Max on the way to her bedroom. Jean shorts and a T-shirt would be her preferred outfit. Instead she put on a flower-strewn sundress she'd purchased on a mother-daughter shopping spree. Her mother always dressed like a fashion ad and never could understand why her daughter didn't do likewise. Before, she told her mother it wasn't practical since her clothes could be stained with tempera paint, clay, or something else equally bad. Now, her excuse would be she didn't want to stand out, she needed to blend in, but today she'd make her mother happy.

She slipped on sandals with a tiny heel. Unlike her mother, she could never manage walking around in stilettos. Max padded into the bedroom and peered up at her with expectancy. What did he want now? "What?"

"Will there be bones there? Big, juicy, meaty bones?" His tongue lolled to one side and his eyes glistened with expectancy.

"Only if they're shaped out of tofu." Her mother's latest health food kick made her nostalgic for the days when they dined on fried chicken from the Colonel, but even he had gone to the dark side by offering grilled chicken.

"What's tofu?" His head turned sideways as he offered a quizzical gaze.

"Lord only knows. I've been told it's soybean curd, but it has the consistency of rubber."

"Yuck!"

"My feelings, too."

"Can we stop by the drive-through on our way there?"

Nala almost asked if his former owner had been a man. She thought one had been, but there were too many others to keep up with. Mentioning it would only bring up bad memories. "A cheeseburger might not be a bad idea considering my breakfast."

"Yay!" Max twirled in a circle, his nails making a skittering sound on the wood floor, possibly scratching it, which would make her damage deposit history.

"C'mon, enough with the victory dance. We need to get going." Nala walked to the front door, grabbing her purse in the process. When she opened the door about a foot, a black bullet shot through it, trampling her toes in the process. Geesh, someone needed his nails trimmed.

Max milled around the car waiting to get in. At least, she still held a modicum of control by being the one with opposable thumbs. "Okay, buddy. I'll let you in, but remember no nose art."

Instead of answering, the dog shot her an aggrieved look. *Weird.*

Her elderly neighbor was out watering her flowers and shouted out a greeting to Nala. "I see you have a dog. A big one, too. A girl needs company."

"Oh yeah, company." She forced a laugh, thinking it was a joke, but realized it probably wasn't.

Once in the car, she rolled down her window to wave to her neighbor. As the car crept down the street, she found herself waving at some other residents and calling out greetings. Max sat up straight, looking ahead, and acting as if he didn't hear the little dogs yapping at him. At the stop sign that led to the main street, Max heaved a heavy sigh.

"Something wrong?" Even though she wasn't too sure of the canine's age, she'd place him at the dramatic teenager stage. All the jokes, eye rolls, smart aleck remarks, demands, and sighs made it seem about right.

"I was hoping to get that cheeseburger this century."

"Yeah, yeah, I know, but I've got to work the neighborhood. I can't just rush through it."

"Why not? Especially since you're trying to get some place."

This wasn't the first time she'd heard this argument, but with people she seldom bothered to explain. Max needed to understand since he'd be living here. "It doesn't cost anything to be friendly. Besides, I learn a great deal from my neighbors. Each one is another set of eyes and ears. They could be part of my investigative network.

"An outdated part."

"You'd be wrong." She shook her head. "Mr. Johnson who sits in his garage every day in his lazy boy chair listening to his radio was the one that told me the empty house down the street was bought by a nurse from New York. Many have information that was never written down. Some of them remember what streets used to be named or who ran what business. This is important when you're following a trail that has gone cold."

"If you say so. I'll settle on using my nose. If a trail gets too cold, it's a sign to give up."

Obviously, Max wasn't an optimist, but why should he be considering his life up to now? She smiled at her companion. "I'd like you to be positive for once."

"All right, if it means so much to you. I'll be positive when I get a cheeseburger."

Dog ownership and being a preschool teacher had a great deal in common. She wasn't sure if she was cut out for either one.

Chapter Fifteen

HER PARENTS' NEIGHBORHOOD had matured rather like its longtime residents. The lawns, which formerly sported bald patches from children's playing patterns or bicycles, now had a deep green and uniform density courtesy of a lawn service. Even though the original houses were modest ranches, they'd changed over time, growing wider with additions. A few even sported a second story. Nala knew better than to mention her observation aloud. It would set her mother off, possibly on a house hunt or at least a makeover.

Several times, her mother, inspired by home shows or by a friend's move, rallied for them to move to a trendier neighborhood or a gated community. This sudden inspiration to trade in what they knew for a place with a commons and a clubhouse was always shot down by her father. He was a fan of sticking to the familiar, at least when it came to houses. They never moved, but her mother would get to redo a bedroom or add a bathroom. After the Homerama, they enlarged the deck and added a hot tub. Too bad all the fun updates happened after Nala moved out.

The green, well-cut lawns boasted a few flowers near the mailbox or bordering the walk. Not so with her parents' home that looked like a centerfold from a garden magazine. People would assume Gwen liked to garden. She didn't, but she did like being the showplace of the neighborhood, which meant both her parents put many hours into the yard. The day lily mound was an explosion of yellow, orange, and red blossoms, but that wasn't what caught her eye.

A shiny, navy SUV sat in the driveway on her father's side. He must have bought a new car. "New car, Max. That causes problems."

"Why?" He leaned against her to see the vehicle. "Looks okay to me."

"The fact it's new means Dad won't let me drive it. He's never forgiven me for wrecking his Mustang Cobra when I was sixteen."

"You wrecked his car? Maybe he shouldn't have let you drive it."

"I didn't exactly ask to drive it." She shrugged and winced, thinking about that night.

"You stole it?" Max's inquiry came out on hot, stinky dog breath.

She gave him a shove back to his side of the car. "Stole is such a harsh word. Although, he did think it was stolen and put an all-points bulletin out for it. When I saw police lights behind me, I pulled to the side of the road, overcompensated, and hit the guard rail." She gave an all-over shudder. "Still, don't like to think about it."

"You were bad."

"Was not."

Her father came around the side of the house and peered into the car. "Who are you arguing with?"

"No one."

Her father raised his eyebrows and waited as he always did when she was lying.

He'd expect something, so she might as well fess up. "I was arguing with Max." She gestured to her canine.

Instead of laughing, her father's brow furrowed. "Gwen was

right. I didn't want to believe it."

"What are you talking about, Dad?" If it involved her mother, she wasn't sure if she wanted to know.

"Forget about it. Your mother is having dinner alfresco, which means we don't get to use the lawn furniture, which your mother had to have and was made specifically for her. Oh, no, Tyler and I had to wrestle the dining table outside so your mother could dress it up with linens, china, and flowers to look like something she saw in a magazine."

"Sounds fancy." She opened her car door and climbed out. She glanced in the direction of the nearest neighbor. "I thought Tom was your neighbor."

Her father did the honors with the other door, releasing Max, who charged ahead to the backyard, probably following his nose.

"He is. Why?"

"You said something about Tyler helping you with the table." She tried to run after her dog, mentally picturing him with his paws on the tablecloth and helping himself to potato salad or whatever else was on the table. "Max, wait!"

Her father grabbed her arm, stopping her. "I need to talk to you."

"I'll make a fuss over lunch and the table and everything, just enough to make Mom happy." She tugged at his grasp, but he still hadn't let go. "What is it?"

"Go ahead and make a fuss, but I thought you needed to know we have company."

"Company?" She repeated the word as if she'd never heard it before. Her parents never invited anyone else to Sunday dinner. When she had been involved with Jeff, they made a point of not inviting him. Why would they invite someone else to an intimate family function? Better yet, who?

Max returned with an attractive man, with a military haircut, strong jawline, and who filled out his clothes very well, holding his leash. His eyes were amused, even if he managed to silence any actual laughter.

"I saw your partner in crime and figured you couldn't be far behind."

"Officer Goodnight?"

"In the flesh."

Her father moved closer, slapping the man on the back while he beamed at his daughter. "Have you met Tyler Goodnight? He's been on the force less than a year."

"Oh, I believe we did meet. Where was that?" Would he try to protect her or finger her as a threat to humanity?

His eyes rolled up as if considering what he might say, then he smiled. A beautiful, wide smile that didn't hint at subterfuge. "I believe you were walking your dog and taking photos."

"That's right," she agreed before he could add any more. "You were very helpful telling me which lens to use for the Masonic Lodge photo."

No real reason to look at her father to see how he was reacting to their conversation. His analytical mind had already recorded it and even now had discovered issues with its presentation.

"I bet Mother's getting impatient since she's been waiting on me. The vegetable skewers might be getting too done. You know she hates that."

Her father laughed. "No worries. I decided to pick up lunch at the Rib Shack since Tyler was coming. Figured he might want some guy food."

"Yippee!" Max exclaimed, but all eyes were on Nala.

Tyler was the first to speak. "How did you do that? Make it sound like the dog was speaking?"

OH, GREAT. HERE was an eligible man who obviously passed her father's inspection, and she would ruin it all by admitting Max could speak. Since she'd already sworn Max to be on his good behavior, he wouldn't say anything. The thought of possible bones must have caused his loose lips. Nala managed a mysterious smile. "Trade secret."

Tyler smirked. "I don't give up easily."

Before she could answer to the flirtation in his tone, her father interrupted. "You must have some device on you. You push it whenever you want the dog to say something. You wait until he has his mouth open so it will look natural."

Even though Tyler had the leash, Max bumped up against her and looked up at her with a questioning expression. "That's it, Dad. You found me out."

"Ha! Thought you could fool your old man. Maybe you could do some more of that. It would really impress your mom."

Nala wouldn't bet any money on that, especially since her mother would already be upset about having her planned meal upstaged by The Rib Shack. The Sheraton table her mother took such pride in looked incongruous next to the pool. That was another fun thing they got after she reached adulthood. Her father liked to tease her, telling her if they got the pool before she'd moved out, she would still be living there.

Instead of Great-grandma Elinor's lace tablecloth, there was a plastic tablecloth covered with daisies. The regular lawn furniture had been moved to a corner. The three chairs would have never worked. Something had happened to the fourth chair. She couldn't remember what.

Gwen stood by the decorated table in her stylish apron that picked up the colors in her floral top. "About time you got here. I'm reheating the ribs since they've gotten cold waiting on you. What took you so long?"

While she hadn't rushed, it hadn't taken that long. Everyone's eyes were fixed upon her waiting for an answer. Too bad she didn't have one. Improvise. "Max couldn't decide which collar to wear."

As if they planned it out, Max responded, "Complain, complain, complain."

"Ah, that's good." Her father slapped his hand against his thigh. "Do another one."

She caught Max's eye who managed the slightest head nod, then he looked down as if embarrassed before uttering the familiar phrase. "Wi Wuv Wu."

The entire group chuckled while Tyler, who was closest, nudged her. "Great one. You're killing it. How about another one?"

Max managed a doggy expression of glee that hinted at another cheesy line. It was hard to tell what he might say next. "Umm, I think that's enough of the dog and pony show." She ignored the lifted canine ear. She'd explain the expression later, once the two of them were in the car alone and headed back home.

Nala turned to Tyler and managed a smile, which wasn't hard since he was very easy to look at. A dimple in his left cheek peeked out at her when he grinned back. Nala asked, "I want to know more about you. What made you decide to join the force?"

Her father echoed the sentiment. "Yeah, I never got the full story. I'd love to hear it."

"Not much to tell." His shoulders went up in a shrug. "As you know I was in the service. Served in Iraq and Afghanistan."

Spencer, her father, interrupted him by holding up one finger. "What was your MOS?"

"Helicopter mechanic, but on my first tour they decided I needed to be more of a policeman supervising the civilians. While most of the other guys who were told their job, position changed to meet the needs of the Army weren't on board with it, I found I didn't mind helping the people, even if I was digging for information on insurgents at the time."

Her father moved to her other side, boxing her in and giving her a slight elbow in the ribs. "Sounds a bit like Intelligence or a bit like being a private eye, huh?"

Nala recognized the comment was for her, but wasn't sure if Tyler did. After all, she'd never explained what her job was. Before she said anything, the handsome veteran answered.

"I wouldn't call it intelligence exactly. All the soldiers were expected to keep their ears and eyes open. Often information came from not so much of what was said, but in what wasn't. When asked if they had seen a known insurgent, an outright forceful denial meant the person was most likely in hearing distance."

Spencer grunted in agreement as Nala stored the tidbit away. "What do they say if the guy isn't in hearing distance?" The information might not be useful in the States, but you never knew. Could be people were the same all over.

"Sometimes the people would go into detail about the insurgent depending on how they felt about him, especially if their family had suffered at his hands. Other times, they might be closemouthed because the person we were looking for could be a cousin or such." He raised his eyebrows and added, "Most of the time family protects family."

"On that note," her mother added, as she carried out a large platter of ribs, "it's time for the family and guest to eat. Nala, go get the corn on the cob. Spencer, grab the rolls and the baked beans."

As Nala walked to the kitchen, Tyler asked if there was anything he could do. Her mother turned aside his offer with a comment about him being a guest. True, but she also knew Gwen Bonne didn't allow strangers into her kitchen, her inner sanctum. Her family she had trained to put everything in its proper place, keeping it photo ready. Of course, that would depend on someone making his or her way into the kitchen to begin with.

The steaming corn sat cradled in a large oval bowl while the baked beans perked in the loaf pan centered on a burner. Nala picked up the corn but had to warn her father, who had donned a hot pad to pick up the beans. "You know you have to pour them into the dish on the counter."

"Yeah, right." He changed his voice to a more formal tone reminiscent of a PBS announcer describing the grand estates of England. "Gwen Bonne never uses a pan as a serving bowl."

Picking up on the banter, Nala attempted an English accent. "Nothing as pedestrian as a pan would ever be seen on the exquisite dining table."

They both smirked at their silliness, knowing the subject in question would not be amused. Nala held the crystal butter dish with her left hand and the corn with her right. "Dad, why did you invite Tyler to lunch?"

He raised his eyebrows and twisted his lips a little. "I have to say, I hadn't thought of him since he graduated. He's not one to cause trouble and doesn't need any guidance. He does his job, but when you mentioned him, I remembered he first came here from Cincinnati since there was no opening in the academy there. IMPD offered him a job before he graduated. No family here. I thought it might be nice for him to have a family dinner."

Her father could be thoughtful. It wasn't too far-fetched that he thought Tyler might enjoy a homemade meal even if it wasn't totally homemade. It still smelled like a fix-up to her, but she'd had worse.

Dinner went amazingly well despite her father and Tyler talking shop. Her mother kept most of her comments low-voiced so the men couldn't hear. "One of my friends who saw you at the mall told me you were a blooming mother."

Her eyes rolled up, aware that was coming. "It was my disguise."

"I suspected as much. I didn't say anything since it was Doris Ledbetter. I only see her every couple of years. Maybe next time I see her I will have an actual grandchild instead of a cotton-padding baby bump."

No way she'd address that. Tyler requesting more potato salad kept her hands busy. With any luck, her mother would move on to a different subject. Anything else but discussing grandchildren would serve her well. Inhaling through her nose, she reached for her happy place. Gwen punctured her tranquility with a gesture to Tyler.

"The veteran-turned-cop is Spencer's favorite. I see you're keeping company with someone named Elvin. Why haven't I heard anything about him? Makes inviting Tyler over here awkward."

Inviting Tyler was awkward, but she needed to clear things up before it became even more complicated. "Elvin is a subcontractor. We'll be working together."

"Working together?" Her mother gave a disbelieving snort. "Yeah, that's what I did with your father."

"When was that?" She couldn't remember anything about her parents ever working together. It would be hard to imagine Gwen in law enforcement and just as hard imagining her father in anything else.

Her mother's lips tipped up in a sly smile. "Oh, when we were making you."

"Argh!" She was sorry she asked.

Chapter Sixteen

THE SUN'S INTENSITY caused Nala to look at her watch. The white-gloved hour hand rested on the three. The Mickey Mouse watch had been a gift from her father on her tenth birthday. It had been more of an apology. Her father presented her with the watch while her mother bought her the complete collection of Disney princess movies. As she remembered it, she'd asked to go to Disney World on her birthday. Since she was born in the summer, it was entirely doable.

Not that summer. She remembered her mother explaining she had a big-deal corporate client while her father was involved in an undercover operation, which explained his scruffy beard. Although, he may have told her that after the criminals were caught. Even family could be an informational leak. At the time, she was bummed, swearing never to ask her parents for anything, ever. That lasted about a week until she wanted to be driven to the skating rink.

It explained why her parents were so over the top now about everything. Somewhere along the line, they realized no more kids were coming and time was running out. Make memories now or else. Well, at least that was how it felt to her. She wasn't sure when the switch happened. It just did. More likely, their careers became established and they could delegate work. Could be the reason her father chose to train recruits. He never got a call in the middle of the night to teach a hostage negotiation class.

Her father and Tyler were still talking, although they had moved on to football. Her mother leaned over and whispered in her ear. "Looks more like they're a match than you two."

The words only confirmed her original thought that it had been a fix-up. She scooted out of her chair, which grated a little on the patio bricks, and stood. "Let me help you clean up."

"That would be nice." Her mother managed an impish look by raising her eyebrows and rounding her mouth. "We could gossip in the kitchen."

About what was her first thought, but she knew. If her father thought he had *interrogation* skills down pat, he could learn a great deal from his elegant wife. Her mother usually had her confessing to things by using the worst-case scenario technique. If Nala had stayed out past her curfew, her mother would imply that a reliable source fingered Nala and Karly as the culprits who toilet papered the geometry teacher's home.

Nala would defend herself by saying she couldn't have done it since she was still at Pizza Village chatting with Ryan, the school's number one hottie, who she bumped into when she and Karly were ready to leave. Unwittingly, she'd confessed to breaking curfew. Her mother probably already knew. The alarm system her father installed recorded whenever she punched in her entry code.

Her mother picked up their plates and nodded at the men at the other end of the table. Nala removed her father's plate without causing the slightest hitch in his rant about how the Colts football team should be run. Tyler glanced up and murmured, "Thank you."

His liquid-brown eyes and warm expression caused her to hesitate for a second, but she responded with, "De nada."

Really? De nada. What was she, a West Coast hipster? She carried the plates crowded with rib bones to the kitchen. One bone tumbled off a plate, and Max was on it in a flash. He dashed to the grass with his bounty as if afraid Nala would wrestle it from him. *Weird.* Typical dog behavior, but most of the time she didn't think of Max as a dog, more of a friend. Could her mother be right? Her failure to form a long-term relationship had turned her into a dog lady. Nah, couldn't be.

After leaving the dirty dishes on the counter, she returned for the serving bowls. The pool shimmered in the sunlight, teasing her. A swim would be nice. She kept an extra swimsuit at the house for such a purpose, but no way would she don it and get into the water with Tyler present.

Most women knew you didn't trot out the swimsuit until you were secure in the relationship or you had a swimsuit model body. If the latter were the case, you took every opportunity to wear a bikini even if it was to pop into the local grocery. She'd spotted a few such women, who possibly delighted the bag boys but pushed the store manager into furtively whispering to the exhibitionists that more clothing might help.

Unless Tyler left soon, she'd have to head home and see what Elvin had for her. Her mother glanced up from rinsing the dishes before she loaded them into the washer.

"What have you found out about Marvin? Have you located his piece on the side?"

She groaned. Here she thought her mother was going to delve into her lackluster love life, but she was more interested in her clients' business. "Mom, I told you I can't talk about it. Discreet inquiry means just that."

"Hah!" Her mother placed a few more plates into the dishwasher before turning with a determined expression. "Beverly is my best friend. We've been friends longer than we've both been married. It's my job to look after her best interests. It might be time to call in a forensic accountant to make sure Marvin isn't shifting money into overseas bank accounts." She wiped her hands on her ruffled apron, then formed a fist and shook it. "We need to slice and dice the man before he heads off to Aruba with his high school bimbo."

That escalated in a hurry. "Mother, he doesn't have a bimbo. As far as I can tell the man is either painting or taking dance lessons. He might even be taking flying lessons since he keeps going to this building next to the airport." Oops. Her mother did it again. The worst scenario trick and she fell right into it.

Gwen tapped her cheek with a manicured index finger. "Bev didn't mention any painting supplies and she has been checking receipts and credit cards. It could be dance lessons. Odd, he never mentioned it. As for the building near the airport, the only thing I know they do there are those training seminars for people who are afraid to fly."

Ding! Nala could visualize a bell ringing over her head. "Marvin is afraid of flying."

"That's what he says." Gwen wrinkled her nose as she continued. "Some men say stuff like that to keep from taking their wife on a desired vacation."

"I know good and well that you and Dad have taken several vacations that involved flying."

"I wasn't talking about your father. The real question is why is Marvin trying to conquer his fear of flying now?"

It seemed self-evident. "He wants to fly."

"Yes, but with whom?"

Her mother wasn't giving up on the cheating husband theory.

"Still, it could be something else. I need to check out the building and wanted to use Dad's old beater truck."

Her mother bent to insert the detergent pod into the dishwasher but turned her head in response. "Keys are on the key ring board by the garage. I have my doubts if it will start. I keep urging your father to take it to the scrap yard if only for the metal. Why not drive your car? It's in better condition."

"I don't want to be noticed." It was the truth.

"Ha!" Her mother smirked. "You think driving a truck whose gears grind and squeak and belches black smoke won't draw attention?"

Nala hadn't remembered the truck being that bad, but she hadn't used it in quite a while. "It's better than my bug. A security guard stopped me for lingering too long near the airport. I played the ditsy female card."

"For shame."

"What's worse is he had no trouble accepting it. I can't show up with the same car, or he'll get suspicious. This time I'll pull into the lot." Her initial scheme to send Max into the building had failure written all over it. What if Max couldn't get into the building? If she opened the door to let him in, she couldn't claim she was chasing him. There was something about a woman chasing a large German shepherd mix through the lobby that didn't fall under discreet inquiries.

Her mother waved her finger. "Rent a car. It would look natural, as if you were returning it to the airport. Fill up a large business envelope, pop into the lobby on the pretense of delivering something. In fact, it wouldn't hurt to have some courier service jacket made up. It would be a fantastic way to get into places. Make sure to use a name not already in use. That way they can't check it out. Even better, some hard-to-say name, which would be difficult to remember."

Her mother appeared to be better at the private eye business than she was. Then again, Gwen Bonne excelled at whatever she did, but she didn't have the services of Elvin the hacker and the possibility of Harry's assistance. Her office friend hadn't come right out and offered to help, but she had a feeling he might. "That's a good one. I should go home and get right on it. Maybe I could get some of those magnet signs you put on car doors to explain my appearance in various places."

"You need a different car. Something like a white sedan. There has to be hundreds of those on the road."

"Don't I know it?" The memory of trying to follow Marvin's ubiquitous white car confirmed her mother's declaration. "Still, a car would be a major business expense."

"Lease one. I know it isn't cheap, but having someone recognize you every time you showed up in your bug won't work, either. You'd have to park blocks from whoever you're watching. Why don't I ask around? I'm sure someone has an unremarkable sedan for sale?"

Deep breath. Nala inhaled through her nose and held it for a few seconds. Her mother would track down a suitable car just because she set her mind to it. Feeling calm and somewhat centered, she decided to put the brakes on her mother helping.

"Mom, I appreciate your help." How could she make her refusal sting less? The only person she knew more driven than her mother had been Grandma Luci, her mother's mother. "Did your mother have any opinions about you running Posh Interiors?"

"Did she?" Gwen's eyes rolled upward. "*Opinions* is too gentle a word. She predicted Spencer would dump me for a co-worker since I spent more time at work than home. You'd become a shoplifter who ran through a series of bad-news men without constant maternal supervision and proper role modeling."

That last part was true if it translated to her being fooled by men who were little more than surface charm. After a while even the surface charm wore off, leaving her confused about whatever she had found attractive.

"Well, Dad is still around. I haven't been caught shoplifting, yet."

Her mother grabbed a dish towel and snapped it in her direction. "Don't even joke about shoplifting. It's an officer's worst fear to have a family member arrested."

She doubted it was the worst one. Being shot had to nudge its way ahead of Aunt Ethel being picked up outside the Dew Drop Inn after one too many Gin Rickeys. "No worries, since I shop online mostly. Not sure how I'd shoplift unless I lifted someone's credit card number."

"Not funny." Her mother narrowed her eyes.

How did they get so far from the point she was trying to make? "I know Grandma Luci meant well."

Her mother snorted as she corralled the empty takeout cartons and trashed them. "Thought she knew everything. Figured I would fail. Wanted to scare me into doing what she wanted me to do."

It did sound rather familiar, although she considered her father was the one betting on her failing. Her career switch didn't change her parents' behavior. Her father thought she should sit down her rowdier preschoolers' parents and explain how their children would be dead or in prison before twenty. Her mother's idea of recording the reprehensible behavior for the parents to witness did improve two students' behavior while another parent threatened to sue until she found out children could be filmed in a public setting for noncommercial purposes.

"Grandma Luci is proud of you."

Her mother pushed her shoulders back and pushed up her chin. "She is now, once I proved myself."

"That's what I'm trying to do." There, she'd said it. The world hadn't ended.

Her mother gave her an indulgent smile and patted her cheek as if she were five. "Of course, you are. That's to be expected. It's also natural your father and I want to help when we can."

Talk about a wasted conversation. "I'll grab the keys and be on my way. You can make my goodbyes to Tyler." Even though the handsome veteran-turned-cop appealed, it would just feel like he was her father's choice and not her own. Too bad, she had to shelf him before she even exchanged more than a dozen words with him.

Her mother's dramatic sigh forced her to ask, "What's wrong?"

"I told Spencer you wouldn't be okay with him inviting Tyler over. He insisted you two already knew each other. The fact you even mentioned him to your father meant you wanted him to arrange a casual date between the two of you."

"Oh, macaroons!" She threw both hands up in the air. Best to leave now while she had her temper under control.

"Watch your language, young lady. Spencer told me what all those cookie names mean."

"Good, because I've forgotten. I don't know where Dad gets his ideas from. Wherever it is, he needs to stop."

"Told him as much."

"I need to leave with as much of my dignity as I have left." She kissed her mother, but decided against saying goodbye to her father. Keys in hand, she headed out the front door. A major scene averted by not saying goodbye to her father and Tyler. The only problem was the missing dog. She whistled. No response.

Even though Max could talk, it didn't guarantee obedience. Instead, he'd tell her why he didn't want to do something. Nice, he didn't want to leave. She gave another sharp whistle. Max rounded the corner with his teeth firmly clamped on Tyler's pants legs.

What was her dog up to now? "Max! Stop! Release!" He did neither. Tyler stumbled along as Max continued to pull on his pants.

"Did you train your dog to apprehend? He'd be great on the force."

Nala managed an apologetic smile, thinking he wouldn't be a hit on the force especially when he started telling people they were doing things wrong. "Sorry, I don't know what's gotten into him."

"Maybe he had some objections about you sneaking off without saying goodbye." Despite having been tugged the distance of the side yard, Tyler patted Max on the head.

"Not sure what goes through Max's mind. I've been alerted to my father's machinations, though. I'm sorry if he invited you over so he could check you out."

Max released his grip on the officer's pants, sat, and grinned at her as if pleased with himself. Geesh, he might not only be a talking dog but a matchmaking dog too. It made her wonder what Karly had told him.

"No worries. I suspect Captain Bonne knew plenty about me before I entered the academy. No need for him to check me out. On the other hand, I came hoping you'd check me out." He waggled his eyebrows.

It was obvious he was teasing her. "Yeah, about that. I didn't have a chance with my father monopolizing you. I better head out." She turned to go, patted her leg as a signal to Max.

Tyler's touch on her arm stopped her exit as effectively as a red traffic light. "Could we have a replay, perhaps a date? Without your father, of course."

Did she want to date someone her father knew? If he couldn't get the details from her, he'd contact Tyler. It would be awkward. Before she could answer, Max did.

"Yes!" *Bark. Bark.*

"Okay, then." He turned her around to meet his amused gaze. "You're the first woman who has ever answered via her dog. That makes you unique."

"That's me, unique. Do you need my number so we can arrange things?"

He shook his head, his eyes still laughing. "Nope, your father gave it to me. Even if he didn't, I could have looked it up since I already have your driver's license information."

"Goodness, why is that particular tidbit less than reassuring?"

He waved his hand as if wiping away her doubts. "No worries. I don't go looking up the info for every attractive woman I pull over. Just yours."

It made her wonder what he found out. "Should I ask?"

"Not much to tell. No prior convictions. You live in an older, established neighborhood. You're single, a pet lover, obviously." He angled his head in Max's direction. "Up till now, you usually dated beneath you, but I hope that's going to change soon."

"What database did you get that last bit from?" She suspected she knew.

"Your father."

"Fig bars!"

"Excuse me?"

"Never mind, it's another thing you can ask my father. Is there anything he didn't tell you?"

Tyler's shoulders went up in a shrug. "He did tell me about you starting your own PI business, but he didn't tell me your favorite restaurant."

"Mercy. Well, it isn't actually my favorite, but I've always wanted to go." She added a smile, forgetting exactly why getting involved would be undesirable. Besides, dinner was just dinner. Everyone had to eat.

Chapter Seventeen

THE WIND GUSTED through the car windows, blowing Nala's hair and Max's ears back. The radio blared some vintage tunes as the two of them sang along. Well, Max howled as opposed to saying actual words, which was probably just as well since traffic tended to clump up the closer you got to the city. The cell phone should have been masked by all the noise, but Nala chose a cat screech ring tone for Elvin. It was as irritating as the man.

The first *mer-rowl* sent Max into a frenzy. "Stop it, Max!" Unfortunately, she couldn't be heard over the barking. The canine turned carefully in his seat, looking for the source of the sound.

"Max, Max, shut up!" She resorted to shouting, not something she ever liked doing. There were times when she ended up screaming at the preschoolers, especially when Daniel Thurston III's small hand reached for the fire alarm.

Max plopped down in the seat. "You know that was rude. You could have asked in a normal tone."

She grabbed her phone, swiped to the right while talking. "I did."

Elvin commented in her ear. "You did what? Something naughty, I hope."

"Enough. You called me."

"True and with some juicy info on Gordon Lansing."

"Which is?"

"Ah, come on, Nala, you need to be in awe of my research techniques."

Her lips pursed as she blew out a long breath. Before she even asked Elvin to help her, she knew he might be difficult, but she couldn't think of anyone else. "I can't be amazed if I don't know."

"Right, right. Tell me this, how close were you to this Gordon character in the restaurant?"

"Not close enough to overhear their conversation, but close enough to see them. Even got a photo."

"You need to send it to me. As in yesterday."

"I will as soon as I get home. Why did you ask about how close I was?"

"Curious if the man looked to be ninety."

"No way."

"Strange. I found two Gordon T. Lansings. One is ninety and tucked away in a senior care facility. However, the other Gordon is just over six foot, with a striking bearing, similar to a Viking."

"That sounds like him."

"He's also dead."

Nala pulled the cell phone away from her ear and peered at it as if it was malfunctioning, then she put it back to her ear. "Did I hear you right? Dead?"

"Yep, but very quietly. It's all hush-hush."

Max grumbled something under his breath, but loud enough for Elvin to hear.

"Girl, you sound like a chain smoker."

"That wasn't—oh yeah, I keep trying to quit." How many times would she lie trying to protect her dog? "Explain that hush-hush matter. As far as I know dead is dead. It's neither noisy nor quiet."

"That's what most people would think."

"Cut to the chase. You're not being paid by the hour."

He chuckled and then cleared his throat. "The younger Gordon T. Lansing was a hotshot business mover and shaker. He came from old money, which is one of the reasons almost no one knows he's dead."

"Come again."

"Suicide. Supposedly, he got liquored up and crashed his private plane on purpose. The family never put an obit in the paper. Instead, they put out a rumor that the man was on a sabbatical. No one is supposed to know, but the servants talk."

"To you?"

"In a roundabout way."

Somehow, she knew she wasn't going to like it, but she needed to know. "How?"

"I hacked into the Lansing family emails. For good measure, I did the servants, too. The family referred to the plane crash as *the incident* while the gardener griped about having to dig the grave even if he did use a power excavator. The person he wrote to reminded him they were paid well not to talk about it. So, whoever is playing the role of the CEO is using Lansing's credentials and Social Security number."

This was getting weirder and weirder. "It sounds like Lansing had his identity stolen."

"Yes. By borrowing someone's stellar reputation, it was easy for him to weasel his way into Bingham Industries."

"Constance Bingham suspects the man is trying to wrestle the reins of the company from her. In the meantime, he could be diverting funds."

Elvin murmured an agreement and then added, "True. Whoever

this person is could have accessed the deceased Gordon's funds since his family hasn't closed anything out."

"Have you found who the pretender is?"

"Now I see how you're going to be. No recognition of my superior skills. All you want is more, more, more. Send me the photo. I will assume the man is up to dirty dealings and will have encrypted his email. Before you ask about the fingerprints, I haven't heard anything yet."

"I already told you I'd send you the photo. As for the prints, contact me immediately. Wake me up in the middle of the night."

"Is that an invitation?"

"Elvin. Knock it off." She'd fire the man if she had anyone else. Besides, since he lost the bet he was working for free. "Focus." Geesh, she was starting to sound like her father. "Is there anything else you need?"

"Nothing really, it's very minor, but needed."

People accused women of beating around the bush. It would be Christmas before Elvin got to the point. "Come on. I have a call on the other line."

IT WAS A fib, but Nala hoped it would speed things.

"I need to access the fake Gordon's computer from inside the building."

"What? You have to be out of your mind." Did Elvin think he was in the script of some conspiracy movie? She darted a look at Max to see if he was as shocked as she was by the suggestion. His snout rested on the open window edge and his tongue hung out of his mouth as they passed a series of fast food restaurants. He released a long, throaty groan.

"Nala, you got to give up the cigs, although that throat clearing might be sexy under the right circumstances."

An eye roll and a mental directive to get the man back on track occurred simultaneously while she eyed the truck edging up on her rear bumper. Young guy and his girl riding close together. Too close, which meant she needed to speed up. She tapped the accelerator as she answered, "Why do you need to be in the building?"

"It would bypass some of the safeguards. People expect a threat from the outside. It's the whole reason for security software. I have a device I can attach to his computer that will scramble signals, causing his security system to do a cyber chase. While his security chases the digital rabbit, I can stroll through his files."

Elvin did have a point, but she could imagine how Constance would react when she explained she needed to break into Gordon's office, which might not be a problem if there was a pass key the cleaning crew might use. "This device you have, could I get one like it?"

"You could, but I won't tell you where."

"That's mean."

"Hacking is an art. Not just anyone can do it. It takes a special temperament and finesse. Only the—"

Nala interrupted. "I get it. I wasn't trying to cut you out of a job. Just thought it might be handy to have it around. After all, I can't expect you to do everything for me."

"I hear ya" he agreed readily. "Still," his voice took a suggestive turn, "you'd be surprised what I'd be willing to do for you."

Nala stuck out her tongue and made a gagging sound, causing Max to give her a curious glance before returning to his drive-by sniffing. "I'll get back to you after I contact Constance. Talk to you later."

"Don't forget the photo."

"I won't. Goodbye."

Her thumb depressed the power button on the phone to make certain there'd be no chance of Elvin overhearing. "I gotta get my own spy stuff. It wouldn't hurt if I learned how to hack. It would keep me from having to deal with Elvin and all his innuendoes."

A familiar baritone piped in, "Perhaps." He swung his snout back to the window.

"What was that supposed to mean?" Not only did she have a talking dog, but he second-guessed her decisions.

"Umm, nothing." Max continued to look out the window.

Her shoulders stiffened a little. "Come on. It meant something, or you wouldn't have said it." *Good Lord*, she was fighting with a dog. The Romeo in the truck was back on her bumper, demanding all her concentration and defensive driving skills. Unaware of the stress of an inattentive driver practically in her tiny backseat, Max chose that exact moment to explain.

"I can't help noticing you haven't solved any of your cases, yet. You only have two. The way I see it, you aren't using all the tools available."

The truck slid close enough for her to make out the elaborate braids Romeo's girlfriend sported. This was not going to work out well. An empty church lot with a wide entrance might be her salvation. The idea made her chuckle as she tapped the gas and flipped on her turn signal. The man would probably never notice it, but maybe the other motorists would mention it when they filled out the accident report.

Her grip on the wheel became precarious as her hands sweated. Gritting her teeth and tightening her grip, she made a sharp right turn into the parking lot without bothering to slow down. The tires squealed, and Max bumped into the dashboard with a yelp.

The car shuddered to a stop while Nala took a deep breath. *Still alive.* Max gave her a slitty-eyed look.

"It's okay not to agree with me, but no reason to get violent. I may opt to sit in the backseat for safety reasons."

"Oh, Max. I'm sorry." She loosened her seatbelt and leaned across the console to hug her dog. "It wasn't about you. It was the guy in the truck I'm certain would hit me."

"He wouldn't have."

Her arms still around Max, she asked, "You're psychic, too?"

Max gave a few high-pitched barks right in her ear, which caused her to release the dog and resume her seat. It appeared he was smiling, so it could have been canine laughter.

He shook his head, wiggled his shoulders, picked up each paw individually before commenting. "Everything is still working. Although, I do have some doubts about my stomach. We should test it out with a cheeseburger just to be sure."

Before she'd met Max, she'd assumed dogs had genteel, helpful personalities a bit like Lassie in the old television show. She was the lucky one who got the mouthy teenage dog who was always hungry. "Yeah, right. You didn't answer my question."

"Yes, to the cheeseburger?

"I'll think about it."

"The psychic part is a definite no. If I were psychic, would I have been in so many homes where I wasn't wanted?"

That part made sense, although people often thought they wanted a pet only to change their mind when the responsibilities that came with a pet proved too much. "Why did you think we wouldn't be hit by truck guy? You had more faith in his driving abilities than I did."

A sharp bark rent the air. Max continued in English. "I had no faith in his abilities, but a great deal in yours. Out of all my owners, you're the most cautious driver."

The thought of being an excellent driver helped calm her racing heart. Of course, they would be safe. Her father taught her all sorts of defensive driving strategies. She could be in one of those road rallies.

"I'd even go so far to say," Max added, "that you drive like a little old lady."

"Little old lady! I'd like to see a little old lady make that turn I made." She thumped her hand on the steering wheel for emphasis.

Max chose to say nothing, demonstrating either that he had no appropriate rebuttal or realizing often silence could be the best comeback. Snickerdoodles, what if Max was smarter than her? Couldn't be. Still, he had a unique perspective on things. It wouldn't hurt to ask.

The car engine gurgled to life as Max squeezed through the buckets seats to reach the safety of the back seat. Not commenting on his action, Nala made a mental note to buy a car harness for her dog. "So, explain all these tools I have at my disposal."

His head rested on the back of her seat, which meant she got a big whiff of doggy breath with each exhale. "Well, the most obvious is me! I could have sniffed Marvin and told you if he had been consorting with a different female."

"How's that?" If most of her cases were checking up on alleged wandering spouses, a quick sniff test would save her time. Clients usually wanted something more like photos.

"I caught Beverly's scent at the office. Humans have to spend a great deal of time together or rub against each other to get their scent on the other."

"Okay, Max." She held up her hand. "I understand how that part works. Proceed."

"I would identify the various smells to decide if there was something new there."

It made sense, but the sniff test was riddled with issues. "What if Marvin hugged his mother or his adult children?"

"Not a big deal, I can eliminate family since they have some of the same scent markers."

"Families smell alike?" This was not something she'd ever noticed.

"Yes, they do. It is an underlying scent usually carried in the pheromones. I kinda sound like a scientist." His lips tipped up in a wide doggy grin.

"Yeah, you do." Her guilt at him hitting the dashboard caused her to make a detour by the burger place.

"People think animals are stupid, but usually we try not to breed within the family."

"Interesting," she agreed, but she needed more than possibilities. "So, right now, I'm fairly sure Marvin is not cheating. We swing by the airport place and see what is inside the building. I'm sure I can get the receptionist at the arts center to tell me what Marvin is doing. So, how are you going to sniff test him?"

"Easy, you take me for a walk. You know the man's movements. It should be easy to intercept him. He'll pet me because I'm the type of dog everyone wants to pet."

Nala chose not to point out if he were that type of dog he wouldn't have ended up at the shelter. Maybe it was karma. When she first thought about being a private eye, she'd considered a partner. Who knew he'd be four-legged?

"Okay. That just about solves the Marvin job. Although, I admit I was opting for just asking him outright. Not a technique I'd use on strangers, but sometimes an unexpected query produces an honest answer since people don't have enough time to construct a lie. What other tools do I have?"

"Tons. You already know two police officers. I bet either one of them could look up a license number for you."

Nala pursed her lips because she wasn't entirely certain they would. At the present time, she didn't have a plate she needed to be researched. "Maybe. What else?"

"It pains me to say this, but you need a lookout. Normally, I could do it, but as you pointed out, some places are basically unfriendly and refuse entrance to pets unless they're service animals. A dog alone without his human companion wouldn't exactly qualify as a service animal. Ask Harry to help."

Harry had been considerate when she was almost mugged. Nala had already played with the idea of asking him. "Why would he want to help me?"

"Seriously, have you no sense of smell?"

It all came down to smells and food when Max was involved. "As much as I hate to ask, what smell?"

"The man is into you."

Her eyes rolled upward of their own accord. Max was starting to sound a bit like her father, who swore a man would be stupid not to appreciate her upright character and cute as a button appeal. So far, she'd discovered there were quite a few stupid men out there. "If I accept Harry might be attracted to me, you want me to take advantage of his possible interest?"

"Many do."

"I had no idea that being a private eye would mean crossing so many ethical boundaries." The traffic thinned a little as they reached the drive-through. She flicked on the turn signal and made a right-hand turn much slower than her previous one.

Max's panting in her ear reminded her of an obscene phone call. "You need to back off."

He did but continued in an aggrieved tone. "I never told you about the ethical barrier you need to cross."

"Can it. No reason for some fast food worker to hear. They could hear your voice and be convinced I sewed someone up in a dog suit."

"That's sick."

Nala ordered two cheeseburgers without condiments to save the interior of her car. She passed them back unwrapped to an eager Max who inhaled them as she drove. When they were a mile from her house, Max put his head back on her seat.

"As I was saying before my delicious snack, there are other things you can do to get information. Call up people pretending to be someone else to get info such as a credit agency trying to get proof of someone working, like in that show we watched."

Yeah, television made it look so easy with everyone volunteering clues. "That was an old show. Everybody has caller ID now."

"Hmm." Max pondered that thought for a moment. "Karly mentioned dirt bags who used blocked numbers so you couldn't see their digits to know who was calling."

Nala tapped down her inquisitive nature that demanded to know what dirt bag Karly had been discussing. There was more of a chance she was talking to herself than to the dog. Note to self, she would watch what she said in front of Max since the dog retained it all. "That's true. Then, there are burner phones."

"What?"

"Cheap phones you buy minutes on, but don't have to hook it up to your actual name. I could even put the phone in your name."

"Not a good idea. I'm better known than you might think."

"You don't even have a last name."

"I do. It's Max."

"That's your first name."

"Nope, my last. The first is a rather rude expression that I care not to use."

Nala nodded, picturing a frustrated former owner screaming at Max for getting in the garbage, chewing through a laptop cord, or ruining the rug. "Yeah, I can guess. I wouldn't make that my burner phone ID. That's another thing on my to-buy list. Right now, I need to email the photo to Elvin. Then we can comb the internet for spyware."

Instead of replying to her suggestion, Max howled as a pickup truck with a barking dog in the back flew past her on the left side of the road. That happened to her a lot. She thought someone was listening to her until they proved they weren't. Upstaged by a dog barking in the back of a pickup truck. *What next?*

Chapter Eighteen

CHASING MAX DOWN the street while her neighbors watched from their lawn chairs in driveways and breezeways was so not on her to-do list. A few even shouted comments, usually about the dog winning. Unfortunately, the pursuit of a cat superseded her commands.

Nala jogged after the two animals, but realized after a couple blocks, she'd never catch up and returned home. Max should know the way back. After all, there were all those stories about pets walking miles to return to their former home. Quite a shock for the person who gave them away.

In the house, she pulled up the photo taken in St. Elmo's bar. The one of her grinning wasn't half bad. She wasn't going to use it as a profile pic since it would involve explaining the details behind it. Her mother would ask who she was with, then mention a bar pic showed a total lack of professionalism. No, thank you. That's why she kept the same old profile image she'd had for the last five years.

The desired image showed Gordon and his guest. They were a heartbeat from turning her way, but her phone captured the picture without any blurriness. The man reputed to be Gordon was handsome, almost to the extent of being movie star stunning, which begged the question of why he tried so hard not to be photographed.

Most men would have posed for numerous shots. A few would have thought of a reason to pull off their shirt, too.

The possibility of a shirtless shot had her thinking about Tyler Goodnight. Yeah, if they ever decided to do one of those fundraising calendars and put Tyler on it, she'd buy one, which would probably be as close as she'd get to the man considering all the awkwardness at lunch. Her talking dog ventriloquist act might be suitable for children's parties, but was just bizarre everywhere else. Then, there was the fact her father talked to Tyler the entire lunch. Most fathers would extol the virtues of their daughters. But instead of talking about how intelligent and resourceful she was, he'd probably trot out the nugget about how she wet herself the first time she shot a gun. That would make an impression. Dad would probably forget to mention how young she was and that she gulped down a thirty-two-ounce soda before hitting the firing range. Nope, she'd never see Officer Goodnight again unless it was in the official capacity. Just as well. She needed time to consider what had made her fall for Jeff. Once she pinpointed the issue, she'd write it down on sticky notes and post it around the house to keep herself from doing such a foolish thing again.

It didn't take any deep thinking to realize she liked how Jeff looked and how people acted around her when they knew she was dating him. Whenever the man played the jerk, which tended to be several times a day, she reminded herself of all the good things about Jeff. As time went on, it was harder and harder to think of something noteworthy about the man.

Her phone chimed, displaying an unfamiliar number. Should she answer it? It could be Constance or even Beverly asking about their case. She swiped to the right, held the phone up to her ear, and murmured a soft greeting. If it was someone she didn't want to talk to—such as a robo-caller or telemarketer—she'd gently hang up the phone.

"Nala, is that you?"

It sounded like Tyler. How uncanny was that? She thought of him, and he called. Last New Year's Eve, she and Karly had written out an intention list for their ideal mate. Karly insisted on burning the lists, then distributing the ashes on a body of water. Nala had joked about how sneaking across a snow-encrusted landscape to a private pond would end up with the dream man being dressed in a police uniform.

"Yes, it is." The phone tumbled out of her hand, but she managed to catch it with the other one. "Sorry about that. I fumbled the phone. Is it okay if I put you on speaker? Max took off after a cat, and I'm listening for his return."

"Sure. Can't lose that dog since he's the other half of your act."

The man had no clue how right he was, at least about losing the dog. "I'm confident he knows his way home." Putting him on speaker meant she had less chance of dropping the phone. Her hands tended to sweat at the wrong times, usually around dateable men, which was another strike against her. No one wanted to date a nervous Nellie. Even though her father had done his best to prepare her for the force, she worried she might choke at an inopportune time, as if there was ever a right time.

"Unless he encounters the dog catcher."

"Dog catcher! I had no idea. Maybe I should go look for him. I'm being an irresponsible dog owner." She moved into a half-crouching position, ready to race out the door and save Max from the trauma of the dog catcher. Although, knowing Max, he probably had frequent user miles on the dog catcher vehicle.

"Calm down. It's Sunday. The dog catcher only works on weekdays. Wayward dogs get a pass on the weekends. I'm sure if Max is caught, he could talk his way out of it." Tyler's laughter indicated his amusement at the idea of Max speaking.

A slight twinge of irritation crept up her spine. Maybe Tyler Goodnight wasn't as great as she previously thought he was. A ripped body and an engaging smile didn't equate to being her soul mate. If the man couldn't get his head around a real live, talking dog, then he wasn't for her. Then, on the other hand, who could?

"Yeah, I'm sure that's exactly what he'll do. So, why did you decide on Indianapolis?"

"I already mentioned this at lunch. I suspect you weren't listening." His tone sounded amused.

It had never occurred to her that Tyler and her father had included her in the conversation. She did remember her father talking about the Indianapolis Academy having an open spot and Tyler applying for it. It was part of the pre-talk to let her know he was going to introduce a guest into their family luncheon. "My mother was so busy keeping me up on the neighborhood gossip I didn't hear all that much."

"I suspected as much. I applied at the academy." Tyler rehashed what she already knew. Nala took the moment to go through the spy gadgets online. Elvin had mentioned a parabolic microphone.

There was one at an auction site. It mentioned something about children as young as six using it to listen to conversations as far as three hundred feet away. The model holding it reminded her of an actor in an old sci-fi movie. The listening device appeared more space gun than amplifier. Why would parents want their children to eavesdrop on conversations? The fact parents whispered or hid behind closed doors demonstrated they didn't want to be overheard.

One listing featured a recorder that looked like one of those athletic bracelets that measured your steps per day. That might be good. Not too expensive either, so perhaps she should pop for it.

"Am I boring you?"

Tyler's query reminded her she wasn't holding up her side of the conversation. The finger she used to scroll through listening devices pushed down in reaction. Unfortunately, it had been hovering over a *Buy It Now* button. Unlike the traditional image of Millennials as super multi-taskers, she wasn't, although she suspected most weren't that good at it either. There was a parabolic mic in her basket.

"OH NO, YOU aren't. I was just wondering why you chose Indianapolis over Cincinnati." That would show she was listening, sort of.

"I never mentioned Cincinnati."

A bark sounded outside her front door. Max was back in the nick of time. "Do you hear that? My dog is back I need to let him in."

She suited her actions to her words. Max walked around her to reach his water bowl in the kitchen. Nala stared at him and asked, "I don't even get an apology?"

Tyler sputtered on the speaker. "An apology for what?"

Nala picked up the phone and switched it off speaker. "I was talking to Max who decided to chase a cat without a backward look."

"Dogs do that. I'm getting a feeling that you're not really into this conversation or me. Not sure why Captain Bonne invited me over."

"He told me he did it because he liked you. Dad felt you could use a family meal even if it was from The Rib Shack."

"You didn't ask him to do it?" The way his voice slowed and lowered told a great deal.

"No."

"I guess I made a fool out of myself. It's all on me. There are some women who really like a man in uniform, but I guess those females are little more than groupies. I know you're not like that."

The man would hang up the phone on her, thinking she had no interest in him. With her luck, her father would delve into the matter, too. "Tyler, I didn't ask my father to invite you, but I did ask about you."

"Oh." His voice swung upward. "What did you ask?"

She certainly wasn't going to tell him about asking her father to ignore anything Officer Goodnight might say. "Just…if he knew you."

"Why do I think that wasn't the entire conversation?"

Probably because you're a better conversationalist than I am a liar. "I think I hear Max getting into something. I better go check."

"Wait. How about going out with me?"

"Sounds great. Get back to me with a time, preferably during the day."

"The daytime?"

"My work day is reversed. I do most of my work at night. I imagine you have a day off or at least a lunch break."

"I do. Although that wipes out Mercy, which only serves dinner. How about Tuesday at one at Jockamos on Washington Street? Do you want to meet me there or have me pick you up?"

Would she be in the middle of something? Even investigators had to eat. "I'll meet you there. Jockamos at one on Tuesday. Bye."

Max wandered into the room and heard the tail end of the conversation. "You forgot to ask if they had outdoor dining and allowed dogs?"

"You're not going."

His alert canine face drooped. "Are you kidding me? You need me to read the signs between you two. Karly explained to me how hopeless you are about picking a good mate."

"Hopeless. She called me hopeless? I don't remember any man in her life."

"Yeah, she said you would say that, and I wasn't supposed to mention it anyhow."

"What else were you not supposed to mention?"

Max swung his head toward the window, strolled over to it, and pushed the sheers out of the way with his nose. He gave a flurry of barks and wagged his tail violently. Something had him agitated. Nala moved up behind him to see what had caught his attention.

Across the street, her neighbors' grandchildren romped across the fresh-cut grass with a Labrador puppy. "Aw, a puppy! You want to play with the puppy?"

"Forget the puppy. I want the children. They love you unconditionally." He pawed at the glass, making whimpering noises.

Her first response was to point out she'd loved him unconditionally, but had she? Was asking him to keep his comments to himself a tad judgmental? If he did speak his mind, there was a good chance an opportunist might dognap him. Although, people could do so many things with the computer, including making deceased singers into a holograph and having them to continue to give concerts. A talking dog wouldn't generate much fanfare or money. The only way he'd be a novelty was if he were the dead dog of a famous person and could sing.

The summer heat was starting to pick up, but the occasional breeze made the screen doors a better option than the money-hog air conditioner. She opened the front door in passing to get the air circulating and as she approached the back door, childish shrieks rang out.

The shrill voices sounded frightened. Odd considering only seconds ago they were laughing. It must be a game. The sound of adorable puppy yelps mingled with a deep, familiar bark. She stopped in mid-step. "Max?"

No sign of the canine in the living room, but the large front window revealed two terror-stricken children screaming as Max ran in a circle around them. The puppy tried to chase Max while her neighbor held up a broom threateningly.

Oh, no! Nala darted across the street, clapping her hands as she went. "No, Max! Stop, Max!" The large dog slowed enough to give her a backward glance as if to question the command.

She'd reached the other side of the street and grabbed Max's collar. "I'm so sorry, Mrs. Hillcrest. Max just wanted to play with the children. He'd never hurt them."

The woman lowered her broom slowly and managed a nod. "What makes you think that dog wants to play with the children? He acted more like he wanted to eat them."

Great, there went her camaraderie with her neighbors. *Pretend everything is okay.* Nala forced a laugh. "Oh, definitely not. He just ate. I think the puppy made him think he was a puppy again."

Mrs. Hillcrest managed a disbelieving snort, but some of the redness faded from her face. "It was hard to tell that when he came barreling across the street."

"Yes, I know. My fault for not locking the screen door." It never occurred to her that she needed to. The only time she locked doors was to keep things out, not in. "I'll keep it locked in the future to avoid any impromptu play dates from Max."

She handled that well, or so she thought. The real judge would be Mrs. Hillcrest. The woman had her broom end resting on the ground and her shoulders lowered as she shook her head. The children crept closer to Max and looked up at her their expressions uncertain.

"Go ahead. You can pet Max."

They each gave the dog moderate slaps, bearing no resemblance to petting. Why Max wanted to play with children baffled her.

Even her neighbor walked over and scratched Max behind the ears, much to his pleasure. Nala smiled at everyone before awkwardly herding Max home by keeping a firm grip on his collar, which forced her to keep her back bent. Once home, she shoved her wayward dog into the house.

"I thought you liked children."

Max plopped down and turned his head sideways as if he couldn't figure out what she was saying.

"Remember, you said you loved to play with children."

"I do, especially the running and screaming game." His tail thumped the floor for emphasis.

Max really thought he was playing a game. "I'm pretty sure the kids didn't think it was a game. Next time, you have to wait to be invited."

A heavy sigh sounded as his front legs slid out and his head plopped down on his forelegs.

"Yeah, I can sympathize, buddy. The popular girls never invited me to play, either."

Max gave another heavy sigh. "I'm sure this is the part where you tell me you're happy now that you were never invited to the popular girls' parties."

"Are you kidding me? Those were always the best parties. As I grew older and the parties grew wilder, I was never invited because they were afraid my father would bust it."

Max lifted his head a little and managed a grin. "Knowing your father, he would have."

The thought that her parents, or at least one of them, was partly to blame for her lack of popularity had soothed the teenaged Nala's feelings. The current Nala knew nothing good would have come from running with that crowd, even if her father had allowed it.

"In the end, I guess I ended up where I needed to be."

Max barked once and added, "With me."

Chapter Nineteen

TUESDAY ARRIVED BEFORE she was ready for it. Even though Nala woke up knowing this was the day of her lunch date with Tyler, she planned on having plenty of time to glam up. What she didn't expect was on their visit to the mysterious building next to the airport, Max would run away for real. Run away might have been an overstatement since he chased after an unidentified brown, fast-moving animal. After his previous behavior with the neighborhood cat, she should have known better.

With any luck, she'd get home in time to peel off her sweaty shirt and spray on some body spray, never mind the hair and full makeup. "Thanks a lot, Max. I'll stink for my date with Tyler."

Max kept his face to the window as he spoke. "You told me to run away, allowing you to search for your dog, which is what I did. Not sure why you're complaining."

She cut her eyes toward the dog for a second as she maneuvered the car out of the terminal area. "You were supposed to dart into the lobby when someone opened the door, then I would be compelled to follow. Five laps around the parking lot didn't reveal any intel."

"Sez you. What about the guards who came out to help?"

"Oh, you mean those two men who kept yelling at me to do something about my dog, pronto!"

"So, you didn't learn anything?"

Max made it sound like she was the problem. "Okay, hot shot. Since I ruined my chance at finding out what offices were in there, what do you suggest?"

The radio played an old rock ballad as she checked her mirror and eased onto the highway. No comment from her dog, not that she really expected any. Here she thought being an investigator would be easy with what training she had from her father and her ability to deduce who the killer was before the hour-long news magazine show ended. Did investigators have interns? If so, she should have served an internship before tackling the business on her own.

Insurance companies employed investigators. If she got on with one of them, she'd spend most of her time checking out social media sites to see if someone claiming disability was water skiing, climbing mountains, or riding dirt bikes and foolish enough to post it. The insurance company would have all the equipment she needed without her shelling out big bucks. The scenario had its merits, but she'd lose the freedom of being her own boss.

She weighed the two options on her drive home. When the traffic exceeded the speed limit, which was most of the time, she managed to stay in the middle of the pack. It gave her a little extra time. By the time she hit her neighborhood, she still had ten whole minutes to shower and dress, which beat the alternative. Max decided to speak as the car bumped into the driveway.

"Reverse address look-up."

"What?" She wasn't sure what he was talking about since he'd remained silent for the entire ride.

"You put in the address of a place to see who lives there."

"I know what it is."

MAX BOUNDED OVER the console and out the driver-side door as if afraid he might not make it out. He pranced beside Nala, keeping his thoughts to himself until they got into the house.

"Karly used reverse address to see if that guy she likes lived where she thought he did."

"When did she do this?"

Mentally, she shuffled through all the hard-luck men Karly had known. Her best friend had the same approach about men that she did dogs. She loved them because they needed her. Didn't mean they would stay or be good for her—the men, not the dogs.

"While I was still at the shelter, she let me into her office, saying something about me needing to be socialized."

Yeah, that would be about right. "Did she mention if it was the kennel salesman?"

"Nope. All she said was since I didn't have thumbs, I couldn't use reverse address to 'check out where the cute poodle lives so I could plan a cute meet.'"

"She has a point. I guess I could have tried that on the building instead of allowing you to run wild. I'll let you into the backyard, but no opening gates or chasing the neighbor's children. I don't have time to catch you, and you don't want the dog catcher to."

Nala left the back door open in case Max wanted back in while she was in the shower. The reverse address idea stuck in her head. It hadn't been the first time she or Karly used it. Besides confirming where a potential crush might live, it usually let her know if someone else was living there with him, like a wife or a girlfriend. Strange how men sometimes forgot to mention those items.

It would be useful as a basic tool. Most records were public knowledge. Even people who insisted being on the no-call list could be looked up through their address.

Out of the shower, she slipped into a pair of shorts that were neither short enough to be skanky nor long enough to be appropriate for athletic seniors. She teamed it with a complementary top that struck the right balance between flirty and not trying too hard.

Nala yelled out the open back door. "Get in here. I can't leave the door open forever."

A black blob shot by her and launched into a graceful leap onto the couch. "Could you turn it on channel thirteen? My soap might be on."

Instead of informing him that watching a show once did not make it his soap, she powered on the television and turned it to the requested channel. "Okay. No nasty surprises while I'm gone."

"Please." Max rolled to his back and waved his front paws in the air. "Nag, nag, nag. Let a dog slip up once and he never hears the end of it."

No time to debate with a canine if she wanted to make it to the pizza joint on time. It might be okay to be a few minutes late, but any longer and Tyler would leave, assuming she wasn't coming. In the car, the car radio blared something about breaking news at Bingham Industries. Her phone chimed at the same time. Nala pawed through her purse for the device with one hand while keeping her eyes on the road.

"Hello."

"It's Tyler. I might be late. Not too late. Have to do a follow-up on a call."

She knew when she accepted the date that there was a chance Tyler might get called in. "Okay. I can grab a table. Let me know if you're not coming if you find out differently."

"Will do. Bye."

"See ya."

She'd witnessed more than one argument between her parents when her father left for a case, often still dressed in his formal wear. If she decided to date a cop, she knew what to expect. Not that she was dating a cop; it was only lunch. Her lips tipped up at the thought of seeing Tyler. The phone burbled again.

It starts. Nala had the phone almost to her ear, ready for Tyler's work excuse why he couldn't make it, when she noticed the phone number was different.

"Hello. Nala Bonne."

"Thank goodness you answered," a breathy voice said.

Nala had no clue who it was, but obviously whoever it was knew her. "Yes." She was hoping the person would elaborate.

"It's me, Constance."

"Oh. How can I help you?" She didn't have the details on Gordon yet. Enough to push for identity theft, but that didn't carry that much time. A year or more depending on if it could be tied to felonies. Still, something about how the deceased owner of the name died didn't sit right. Maybe Constance wouldn't ask.

"I need help. Goons tried to kidnap me. They forced me into the trunk of my own car. I escaped when they stopped at a convenience store. I know they're looking for me. Right now, I'm crouched behind someone's shed in the Irvington area. I recognized the surroundings since we used to attend the Methodist church located here when I was a girl."

"Did you call the police?"

"The police!" She gasped. "I meant too, but I ended up calling you. You're nine on my speed dial."

How could she best protect her client? "Look around you. How far are you from the church?" Silence made Nala wonder if Constance had been snatched, but if she had, wouldn't she have screamed? The sound of traffic could be faintly heard in the background. Nala tensed, realizing in her present location there was very little she could do.

Finally, the woman spoke in a whisper. "Three blocks. I can see the front door. There's a lot of shops and restaurants bordering Washington Street. Maybe I could walk along the back edge of their property to stay hidden."

"No, you don't want to do that. Being in the shadows will make it easier to be taken. You need to change your appearance if possible. What are you wearing?"

"Slacks, tank top with a windbreaker, sandals. Why?"

"We have to change your appearance. Is your windbreaker reversible?" Nala mentally reviewed how Constance dressed. She couldn't count on her kidnappers not identifying her, but who knows. Minor changes sometimes had an enormous impact.

"No."

"Is there anything around you such as clothes on the line or a discarded sun hat?" It would be a long shot considering no one she knew still hung out clothes.

"No, I don't see anything. Wait. I have sunglasses in my windbreaker. They took my purse, but I had my cell in my pocket. Luckily, my pants are roomy and my phone was off. I never even had time to put on my sunglasses. They grabbed me as soon as I stepped out of the house."

"Alarm system?"

"Disabled, I assumed."

Nala's mind raced as she tried to figure out an escape plan for Constance. "I'm almost there. I was going to tell you to go to the church, but it's a Tuesday, which means probably no one is there. I think you should head for a crowded restaurant. How about

Jockamos? I was heading there originally. Look toward the street, can you see it?"

"Not yet, but I might be at the wrong angle. Let me put on my sunglasses. They're prescription. Ah, now I see it."

"Good. Take off your windbreaker. Untuck your tank top. Mess up your hair. Keep the sunglasses on. I'm driving a vintage blue Beetle. Check to make sure the coast is clear and then run to the busy side of the street. Stroll with some attitude, glance at a few shop windows while being aware if anyone is getting too close to you, then dart into Jockamos."

"Attitude, I'm not sure I have any."

"Get some fast. Hold your head up. Act like you know people want to be you."

Constance inhaled deeply. "I'll try. Hurry."

"Almost there." She checked the street for oncoming traffic and turned on red despite the sign telling her not to. She should have told Constance to call the police. There was a better chance of them getting there faster than she would.

Nala moved her fingers over her cell looking for Tyler's number and pushed it. Instead of the familiar sound of the phone ringing, the sound of traffic poured through her cell. Constance must have forgotten to disconnect. At least she could hear what was happening.

The traffic on Washington Street moved much slower than she'd like. If the driver in front of her would get a clue that if he maintained a constant speed, he could make the lights, she'd arrive much faster, possibly in time to help.

The traffic in the other lane was bumper to bumper, too. Her first real, big-time client might die if she didn't rescue her. Sweat beaded her upper lip as she considered the wide sidewalk to her right. Volkswagen Beetles were known for being able to fit on a sidewalk. She pulled the steering wheel hard in the direction of the curb and had enough momentum to climb it, but could possibly dent her rims.

The few pedestrians on the sidewalk jumped out of her way with a few choice words as she drove slowly and yelled out her open window to alert them. Even in low gear, she was still moving faster than the stalled traffic. Strolling young lovers with their arms around each other's waists halted her progress. Her hand on the horn got them moving and the attention of a few shopkeepers.

Almost there. The sidewalk sloped to allow wheelchairs and strollers an easy descent, which she used to coast back into the lane in front of the inconsistent speed driver who made his protest known with both his horn and voice. She slid into a miraculously empty space in front of the designated restaurant. A woman rushed out and jumped into her car, startling Nala.

Even though she was expecting Constance, the sunglasses-wearing woman looked nothing like the woman who came into the office. A dirt smudge decorated her nose while long, fresh scratches were on both arms. "Let's get out of here!"

In her rearview mirror, a man wearing an apron emblazoned with the name of the restaurant waved his fist in her direction. A stoplight change stopped the flow of traffic and provided the exit she needed.

Her first goal was to get Constance somewhere safe. "Buckle up. After you do that, I need you to call for help. Better hang up, first, though. You left your connection open."

"Okay. Sorry about that." She waved her hands. "Too much happening." She fiddled with her phone. "Done."

The rearview mirror revealed a car a little closer than Nala would like. It didn't necessarily mean anything since traffic could be heavy around lunch time. "Did you say the kidnappers were using your car?"

"Yes, why?" She threw a nervous glance at Nala.

"Would you have a silver Mercedes sedan?"

"I do." Constance took a quick backward peek, then slumped in her seat and wiggled to slump some more as if trying to vanish in the tiny space.

The two tough-looking men in the stolen sedan could have landed jobs as thugs in any crime drama. The man in the passenger seat reminded her of the stranger she'd seen in St. Elmo's. If she were a cartoon character—which would be preferable to real people trailing her with guns that shoot real bullets—a thought bubble would have formed over her head with words that recommended a fast exit. Expensive haircut's profile included mass murder suspicion for which he mysteriously escaped prison time.

Her father would point out that no one was guilty until proven guilty, but kidnapping a woman from her own home and tailgating them said GUILTY in capital letters to her. "Constance, take my phone. She surrendered the cell still clasped in her hand. Hit number three on speed dial for my father. Put it on speaker."

Her eyes were constantly scanning the road ahead looking for stalled cars, bicyclists, children playing near the street, anything she might have to swing around. She'd head to 465, maybe hide behind some semi-trucks, and with any luck, make it to Carmel. There's one thing her car and she excelled at, roundabouts. If the pursuers weren't from around here, and she suspected they weren't, the roundabouts ought to slow them down.

Her father's voice filled the interior. "Nala, what is going on? I've had a report you're driving on sidewalks. A pedestrian snapped your license plate. Elvin is here and insists you're in danger."

"Elvin is there? Never mind. Constance and I are being chased by some guys that tried to kidnap her. They're driving Constance Bingham's silver Mercedes, ah, sedan."

"It's an E-class." Constance shouted from her huddled-up position on the floorboard, then gave the license plate number.

"Got it. Tyler's sending out an APB."

"Tyler's there too? No, never mind. I'm on 465, hoping to play hide and seek using the truck traffic."

"That's not a good idea. You need to let the police handle it."

"I'd like to. Right now, the police need to grab the man calling himself Gordon Lansing."

Elvin's voice came over the speaker. "I showed your father and Tyler the hits I got off the photo you sent me. Gordon is a big deal with Interpol. Big deal in that several countries are looking for him."

Before he could say more, a bullet pierced the back window of the car, spidering the glass and causing Nala to yelp.

Her father's deep voice demanded, "Did I hear shooting?"

"Yes. Can't talk now."

Horns honking and squealing tires signaled the crash of two cars trying to avoid the man hanging out the window, pointing a gun. A large semi-truck lumbered in front of her. The shoulder was narrow, but it looked like her only option since the Mercedes was in shooting range. Constance whimpered, but Nala had to focus.

While other fathers spent very little time teaching their daughters how to drive, Spencer Bonne made sure she could drive both an automatic or stick and could use four-wheel drive when needed. Not only could Nala drive over rough road, she could handle ice and snow like a pro. But one thing her father taught her that she'd never thought she'd use would be put to the test.

The Beetle was practically touching the truck's back end when she swung to the shoulder. A quick correction had her heart racing as she inspected the guardrail much closer than she'd like. The sudden stop stalled out the car. Her breath caught as she pushed in the clutch, moved it to neutral, and restarted the engine, praying it would catch. The car bucked as she floored it in first, again when she shifted up to second. Then third, while rolling along the shoulder looking for a spot between the behemoths of transport. A close spot would keep the sedan from following her, but it wouldn't keep her safe unless a truck was in the second lane, keeping her pursuers from using the Beetle and its occupants for target practice.

A shadow appeared over her car with the chop-chop sound of helicopter blades. Sirens sounded as a fleet of squad cars hit the highway. Her father always joked if anything happened to her that he'd call out the force. Unfortunately, the eighteen-wheelers slowed and cut into the shoulder, making the slender passage even smaller. The alley between the guardrails and the trucks grew narrower and narrower until Nala had to do the thing she hated most. She stopped the car and put it in reverse, watching the rearview mirror for the guardrail, traffic, and potential killers.

The police helicopter dropped low, trailing the stolen car, practically landing on the vehicle. Constance raised her head enough to peer over the edge of the windowsill. "Oh, my car. They aren't going to scratch it, are they?"

Seriously, her car? She was worried about her car. Before Nala could say anything, a police car eased onto the shoulder, stopping her backward crawl. Just as well. She could only reverse so long. She killed the engine and dropped her head back to the seat rest. The cavalry had arrived. As much as she appreciated their presence, she wondered if it would wipe out everything she had done so far. After all, she and Elvin dug up the dirt, and apparently annoyed the vermin while doing so. The police had swooped in when needed and stopped Constance and she from being used for target practice. People tended to focus on the last thing that happened, and not everything leading up to that moment.

All the traffic had pulled to the sides of the road while squad cars flanked the sedan from a safe distance as the helicopter led it off the exit ramp.

SPENCER BONNE SPOKE as he opened her car door. "Glad you're safe. Bet you're grateful now I taught you those defensive driving techniques."

"Yeah, I am. You were right. I did need them." She managed a wobbly smile, which was the best she could do with the memory of almost being shot still hanging on. "Are you good to drive?" Her father's eyes softened as he held her gaze.

"A little shaken, but I'll not leave Sweetie alongside the road. Can we have a police escort?" she joked, trying to demonstrate she wasn't as rattled as she felt.

"Sure, you can. All the way to the police station for a debriefing. After that, I imagine your mother will have her own debriefing complete with food." He nodded in toward Constance, who had inched back onto the passenger seat.

"You're invited."

Chapter Twenty

ELVIN SHOWED UP at the police station, clutching the printouts he'd pulled from Interpol. No one questioned him on how he managed such a feat. Instead, they took the copies he offered that showed the mug shots of the man claiming to be Gordon Lansing. The name beneath the images was Gustav Lang. Nala had to wonder if that was even his real name.

Her father tapped the picture. "The man is wanted in several countries for running scams that separated the foolish and the wealthy from their money."

Constance stiffened up in her chair and pressed her lips together into a pained expression.

"He didn't mean you," Nala said quickly. "After all, you hired me because you were certain he was skimming money from the company."

"True." She sighed. Her hand went to her neck and rubbed it. "I can't understand why my father trusted him? Why so many of the board members thought he could do no wrong?"

"Dozens of people trusted him," Elvin explained as he held out a paper detailing the various warrants sworn out against Lang. "He did a little bit of everything. Look here."

He pointed to some text halfway down the paper. "He posed as a priest and got devout widows to sign away their inheritances to build an orphanage that never got built. In Italy, he ran a Ponzi scheme. He was arrested in France but escaped by telling the police officer he needed to go to the bathroom. He charmed people, even those who should know better."

Tyler joined the group. "We got Gordon—or should I say, Gustav—fleeing the country. Thank goodness for airline passengers with artificial joints. He was already in the security line, but the man in front of him had a hip replacement, and they had to keep wanding him, slowing everyone else down."

Constance pursed her lips. "I'd think with all the money he fleeced from Bingham Industries he could afford a private jet."

"Maybe so," her father continued, "but he might not have been intending to leave right away, especially after he announced your unexpected step-down as the head of Bingham Industries at a press conference earlier today."

"My what!"

The shy, self-effacing female vanished as a livid Constance took her place. Her eyes narrowed, and she shook her fist. "So, this was his plan? Maybe that's what it was all along. He could pretend to consult me on matters as he bled the company dry. I still can't understand how he did it. I considered my father an intelligent man."

An intelligent man who had been thoroughly played, but Nala knew enough not to mention it. The con artist would have killed Constance and buried her in a shallow grave, all the while visiting her house and pretending to relay business details to her. She took a slow look around to see if anyone else had similar thoughts. Her father had that tense action hero set to his shoulders. Her mother swore he could suck in air and inflate his chest and shoulders the way some birds did in courtship rituals.

Elvin clucked his tongue, sounding like a cross between a chicken and a fourth-grader. "Get rid of the real power behind the company. I guess he figured when he couldn't romance you, he'd settle for getting you out of the way."

"Elvin." Nala angled her head in a way that meant *be quiet.*

Instead of being offended, Constance gave a derisive snort. "I had some time while I was in the trunk to consider how my alarm was disabled. All this helpful coming-over stuff usually occurred about the time I arrived home or at dinnertime, which gave the man time to check out the alarm system. I even caught him at the panel once when I excused myself to go to the bathroom. When I refuted his statement about us dating, he never tried to romance me after that."

"Yeah." Elvin directed a devoted look in Nala's direction. "No man would give up on someone he truly cared for."

Oh, snickerdoodles. Say it wasn't so.

Tyler raised one eyebrow and handed a piece of paper to her father, who read it and acted surprised. "It's starting to come together."

"What? What's starting to come together?" Nala rocked to her toes to try to see whatever was written on the paper. The contents of Gustav's suitcase were listed. Mainly he had packed money, lots of it, and a strange list of hard-to-pronounce drug names. She tried to memorize the names.

Tyler folded the paper, tucked it in his shirt, and moved closer to Nala. He placed a hand on her shoulder and gave it a squeeze. "I'm so grateful you're okay. I'd never forgive myself if anything happened to you. As for the date, I understand." He made a sharp pivot and walked away.

Understand what? It felt like she was underwater since she could see everyone's lips moving but nothing, they said made any sense.

A German shepherd rushed into the station trailed by Gwen Bonne. Max thrust his wet nose into Nala's hand, his unspoken question as clear as day to her.

"I'm okay."

Her father mistakenly thought she was talking to him. "I know you think you are, but these things take time. Let's head over to the house. Who's manning the homestead since you're here?" He addressed the last question to his wife.

"Bev and Marvin. When I left, he was waltzing her around the backyard demonstrating his newly finished dance lessons."

So that was the class he was taking at the Masonic Hall. She was right. Call it a gut reaction, but she knew Marvin hadn't been stepping out. Still, it didn't answer where he was going to when at the airport. "You knew he was taking lessons?"

Her mother winked at her. "Maybe."

What else did her mother know? "What is that place near the airport?"

Gwen wrinkled her nose and grinned. "Exactly what I told you, a center for those who are afraid to fly. It helps them conquer their fear of flying."

Something felt like a set-up. "You knew all this, but Bev didn't."

Her mother placed two fingers against her lips. "I was sworn to secrecy." Then, she shrugged.

Nala dropped the conversation, not wanting to say too much more in front of her one remaining client. The fact she hadn't unearthed what a threat Gordon was before he turned deadly made her doubt herself. "Um, Constance, I'm not sure if I should take the retainer you gave me. After all, I didn't do that much."

Elvin cleared his throat and pointed to himself.

"Of course not! You deserve more. Not only did you believe me, but you risked your life. Can't say anyone has ever done that for me."

Well, when put that way, she did deserve the money and the praise.

Her father slipped his arm around her. "I'm very proud of you. Maybe I haven't been as encouraging as I should about your new career. That was all me and my pride. I stubbornly wanted you to follow me into the force. Even though you have no concrete experience as a private eye you have grit and determination. That will take you where you need to go." He gave her a little squeeze before dropping his arm."

The words almost made her tear up. Her father was never a big one for public affectionate displays or speeches, but today he did both.

Tyler's police radio crackled and a code came through for a breaking and entering. The dispatcher repeated the address. It was her building, again. Who knew the biggest mystery she'd have to uncover would involve her own building?

Tyler glanced at her father, who nodded and followed him out.

Her mother elbowed her as the two men walked away. "Let's go check it out. Are we not a mystery-solving team?"

The correct answer was no. There was no team. She was an investigator. Her mother, on the other hand, was an unstoppable force."

The woman in question shook her head. "I want to go. All my life I've played it safe. It didn't keep me from being kidnapped. Why not check it out? Take a walk on the wild side?"

Elvin whooped his approval while her mother gave a knowing

look and jingled her keys. "I'll drive since I have the larger car."

They crowded into her mother's car with Elvin and Constance in the back. Max insisted on being by the window in the front, not leaving much room for Nala. As her mother reversed, Nala turned to share information with Elvin.

"Have you ever heard of scopolamine?"

Elvin gave a long whistle before he answered. "Heard of it. Some call it the Devil's Breath. Heard tales of people giving away their savings to a total stranger without a second thought once they ingested some. Another reason not to take candy from strangers. Why do you ask?"

"They found it in Gustav's suitcase."

Constance leaned forward to grab Nala's hand. "It all makes sense now. Why my father liked Gustav so well. Why the board of directors thought he was the golden boy. Even why my aunt in the nursing home allowed him to manage her shares."

Elvin held up one finger. "Consider the story of the real Gordon Lansing deliberately crashing his plane. Was it suicide?"

Nala sucked her lips in at the possibility. Had she been trailing an international killer without taking appropriate precautions? Worse yet, what about Constance? "Did Gordon ever offer you anything to eat or drink?"

"No. He was always showing up when I was about ready to eat. Brought me wine once, a Merlot. Was disturbed when I didn't open it."

Elvin spoke before Nala could.

"Do you still have it?"

"Yes, I put it in the utility closet off the kitchen. I don't drink Merlot."

The puzzle pieces were starting to come together. Gwen added her comments as she pulled out the police lot. "It sounds to me like he hoped to romance you, which in itself can be a powerful drug. When that didn't work, he brought you tainted wine. It was important that you drank it while he was there so he could make the suggestion. You could have had a glass or two while watching the Home Shopping Network and with your money, HSN profits would have skyrocketed."

Constance's face whitened a little more as she leaned back against the plush car upholstery. "Here I thought the man was just annoying. I never realized how dangerous he was. Kidnapping was his last effort. If all worked out, he could have been a very rich man."

Even though they had caught Gustav, Nala still wanted to lift her client's spirits. She cut her eyes to Elvin, he gave a slight nod and engaged the recent crime victim in playful banter.

Nala turned back around in her seat to talk to her mother.

"Tell me more about Marvin's plan."

Her mother's voice turned soft. "It's so sweet. Marvin wanted to do something extraordinary for his wife, but it involved some effort on his part. He mentioned his plan of taking Bev on a wine and food tour through Italy. I was the one who suggested he should take dance lessons. All the better to dance in the Italian moonlight with his wife."

"What about him smelling like Italian food?"

Her mother laughed. "He told me he couldn't stand Italian food and worried he wouldn't be able to stomach the trip. I told him he'd been going to the wrong places. He needed authentic food. Told him to try out Matteo's in Noblesville."

Nala's nose wrinkled thinking of all the energy she spent trailing Marvin when she would have been much better off trailing the imposter. "Why did you act like Marvin was a deadbeat when you knew better?"

Her mother turned away from the road to arch her eyebrows in her daughter's direction. "Bev was so pleased she wasn't going to have to divorce Marvin. I'm not sure if the fact her husband wasn't cheating or the trip to Italy was the better anniversary present. I have to say my acting skills were stellar."

In her mother's mind, it probably made sense. Thank goodness her mother didn't do marriage therapy. "What about me?" She whispered the words, not wanting Constance to overhear.

"Oh, sweetie, everyone has to start somewhere. I told Bev about your business. I didn't tell her to employ you. She made that decision on her own. Of course, I couldn't say anything. Sworn to secrecy, you know."

It all resembled an elaborate charade she'd played a significant part in. At least it ended well.

Constance spoke from the back seat. "Elvin told me he could do a forensic search on the company's computers and unearth any hidden or encrypted files."

"Do this right away because I still believe Gordon wasn't working on his own. He was the mastermind, but he had his minions. You certainly don't want any of them remaining in your work force. It might even be time for you to take the reins of the company firmly in hand and do a thorough cleaning of those who do not serve you well." Nala suspected any accomplices were well on their way to a tropical hideout, but she could be wrong.

It looked like Elvin was going to get to play with Bingham Industries' computers without dressing all in black. They arrived to find Harry, her office neighbor, standing on the building steps talking to the police. She had to reach across Max to open the door.

The large dog bounded out, but for once he kept silent and padded closer.

Their silent approach was ruined by her mother, who announced, "The gang's all here." And they were.

IN THE SHADOWS between two buildings, Toby watched the people gather around the steps. It looked like a party. His hands balled into fists. The emeralds belonged to him at least in his mind. He deserved them, especially since he'd already done his time. He worked his chin back and forth, considering the situation. No way he was giving up when he was so close. Too many people and all the coming and going wasn't going to work. Businesses started every day and often ended as fast. All he had to do was wait the girl and her dog out. Speaking of dogs, the black beast looked his way and gave a single bark as if he could see him hidden in the shadows.

THE END

Requiem for a Rescue Dog Queen

Book Two of

The Talking Dog Detective Agency

Will be out in October 2017

(Let's check in on Donna and Mark's antics in book seven of *The Painted Lady Inn Mystery Series,* which will be out in August 2017.)

Weddings Can Be Murder

M K Scott

Chapter One

THE TALL PALM trees strategically placed along the Miami shoreline reminded Donna of a former crime show set in a similar locale. Even though it was early morning, many cruisers crowded the deck as the huge cruise ship was guided into its berth. Steel band music played in the background. Mark nodded at the people below them on the next deck. "No one is going anywhere fast."

Heloise spotted them from below and waved with both hands, trying to get their attention. Even though her mother had taken Legacy's best-known gossip under her wing, Donna had more than her share of the opinionated female. She pretended to gaze in a different direction as if missing the woman's flamboyant gesture.

Not easily dissuaded, Heloise cupped her hands around her mouth and yelled. "Donna Tollhouse, I know you can see me! Your mother wants to know if you and lover boy…" Fortunately, the appearance of her mother stopped the ship-wide announcement.

Mark wrapped an arm around her and dropped a kiss on her hair. "How about we just stay on the ship instead of going back to

Legacy?"

"It's do-able, but what about the wedding? I'm sure Heloise has already called in the news." Even though any of her family members who were onboard could have made an early morning phone call once they came into cell range, her money was on Heloise."

"The captain could marry us."

"True." They had played with the idea while sunning on sugar white sand beach. The idea of bypassing the pageantry and trouble associated with weddings appealed to her. However, her hidden soft side relished the possibility of using the silver candelabras and cut-glass punch bowl she'd bought previously at an estate auction. "It might be hard to run a bed and breakfast from the sea."

Mark lifted one eyebrow and asked in a mock serious voice, "Have you considered a floating bed and breakfast? It's bound to be unique."

"Do you think I could jack up the mansion and load it onto a pontoon platform?" Laughter greeted her suggestion, but before her fiancé could offer any alternatives, Security Director Ramirez hurried their way. Even with his olive complexion, his still appeared flushed.

"Mark. Donna. Glad I got you before you disembarked. Your neighbor," he pointed back to Heloise who trailed him, "spotted you from below and showed me where you were. The authorities would appreciate it if you'd do a rundown of everything that happened. Just for the record, of course."

Donna made a dissenting sound that caused Ramirez to explain more. "It won't take long. They only want facts, that's all."

"I'll be glad to help." Heloise had crept close enough to join the conversation.

An urge to be mischievous tempted her. Donna spoke, "That

would be wonderful! After all, you were there for so many of the pivotal events."

The woman practically glowed as she moved closer to Ramirez, talking as she did so. "Well, I knew there would be trouble as soon as I saw…"

Mark and Donna hurried away. They avoided glancing back, afraid an anguished look from the security director might have stopped the escape. Giggling, they jogged down the corridors holding hands, darting around passengers until they reached Mark's cabin. Once inside, Donna slammed the door and leaned against it. "Woo-wee, that was fun! I feel like a kid again.".

"Yeah, I know what you mean." Mark wiped his sweaty brow with his forearm. "You bring out the secret rebel in me."

"Ha!" She moved away from the door to deliver a playful push. "It was always there."

"Hey, I didn't say it wasn't there. I said you brought it out." He blew out a long breath and announced what they both knew was inevitable. "I will have to go and talk to the police about the case. Without our help, murderers and would-be murderers could walk. We will give our depositions, but there's a possibility we will need to fly back as witnesses."

That would certainly throw a monkey wrench into their wedding plans. Should they even plan anything knowing they might get called in as eyewitnesses? She groaned heavily before speaking. "Why is it always so much trouble being on the right side of the law?"

"Don't dwell on it too much. Unless you're planning on a long engagement, we'll be married before it even comes to court. We might end up missing our flights though. I've already been through the rescheduling thing. Maybe they'll give us a break on fees if we explained we're helping keep the cruise lines safer."

Even though it sounded good when Mark said it, she knew the airlines wouldn't see it that way. "I wish. They might view the cruise lines as the competition."

"True enough. Did you put your bag out last night for disembarking?"

The dear, sweet man thought she had only one bag. "Yep, but I still have my carry-on and my tote bag. So, if we get stuck in Miami…" She splayed her hand against her chest as if the idea horrified her. "…I can get by." Personally, she wouldn't mind another day, just her and Mark. Half of the cruise Mark had missed while she was busy being Janice's wing woman and the other half was spent on fingering the killer. Not exactly what she'd call a restful vacation. It would be less stress to get back to the inn.

"Everything I have, except for my sports coat, wallet, passport and airline tickets, should already be on their way to the airport."

While this was her first cruise, she seriously doubted the luggage went to the airport. "Don't worry about it. I met a lady at midnight bingo who always uses a bright yellow suitcase since they line up the suitcases where you came on." Remembering Mark's entry through the Puerto Rican Port Authority, she corrected, "I meant where I came on. Anyhow, the woman joked about people with black suitcases often snag the wrong one."

A pained expression knitted Mark's eyebrows together briefly as he lamented. "I have a black suitcase."

"Oh!" She hadn't thought of that, but men tended to go for the nondescript bags. "Well, surely you tied a colorful scarf on it?"

His disbelieving stare meant no color ribbon and material of any kind was attached to his black conformist suitcase. "A whimsical luggage tag such as a shark or Mickey Mouse?"

"I used the tag that came with the bag. It matched the bag."

She shrugged her shoulders. "Maybe when we're done talking to the police, everyone will have picked up their bags and ours will be the only ones left."

"Let's hope not. I heard a couple up on deck talking about staying onboard as long as they could, which appears to be hours."

A knock on the door stopped their obsession on bags and disembarking.

A voice announced from the other side of the door. "It's Ramirez."

When Mark swung the door opened, the man shook his index finger at Donna. "You did a very naughty thing up on the deck. I will overlook it since you helped me track down a killer."

Helped him? That's not at all how she remembered it. Ramirez accepted that an elderly man, who had access to all kinds of drugs, decided to commit suicide by taking a swan dive from the uppermost deck that had a chest high railing. If that didn't have suspicious death written all over it, she didn't know what did. A shudder passed through her body when she realized it could have ended there. All the cruisers may have been a bit put out that a fellow cruiser had the bad taste to die on their cruise. The memory of the incident would last about ten minutes only to be brought up again when they arrived back home.

Before she could correct his reference to himself helping, Mark spoke. "What can we do for you?"

"It's me helping you." Ramirez used his thumb to point back at himself. "You won't have to go through the protracted process of leaving the ship. I've had your bags pulled out of the baggage area and they're waiting in a courtesy limousine. All we have to do is take the freight elevator and you'll avoid the hassle, give your statement, and make it to the airport before your chatty friend." A flash of white teeth signaled a grin, although his heavy mustache overshadowed it.

Limousine could sometimes be code for *aging white passenger van*, but a ride was a ride. She'd beat everyone to the airport, whiz through security, and be one step closer to home. "Sounds good to me. We'll need to stop by my room and get my bags."

Ramirez held up one hand. "Done. Your kind roommate passed them out to me and they should be on their way to the limo."

Because the man was being super accommodating, Donna's antennae went up. People weren't that nice without reason, which made her wonder what Ramirez's angle was. Mark would probably advise her to wait and see and to stop being so cynical. It's hard to make plans if you don't know what type of ground you're standing on. The best way to deal with the unknown was full speed.

Her lips tipped up into a forced sweet smile that made Mark wince the tiniest bit. "You're being awfully nice to us. Fast checkout, limousine, which is appreciated, which brings me to, what do you want?"

Mark coughed, patting his chest as if all the air in his lungs had just been sucked out. Her eyes stayed on her fiancé and judging by the lack of sweating and redness, she deduced it was nothing more than a distraction.

"A woman who speaks her mind." Ramirez slapped Mark on the back. "You've found yourself a treasure."

After clearing his throat noisily, possibly to make a coughing fit appear more legit, he responded, "I often tell myself that."

She doubted that. There was a good chance the men would waste time exchanging pleasantries and she'd never get an answer. Donna resorted to waving, which was such a Heloise move and she resented having to use it, but it stopped the men from their pointless exchange.

Ramirez nodded to her as if he'd somehow forgotten she was there. "Did you have something to add?"

One hand fisted and ended up on her hip. Some people might call it her *I mean business* stance, but anyone who knew Donna knew it was both hands on the hips that really meant business and not the other way around. "As you know, we're interested in catching our plane. To facilitate everything in a prompt fashion, I need to know what you want." She held up her index finger, "If I don't know, I can't give it."

"Ah, yes," Ramirez's hand stroked his mustache slightly, muffling his reply. "It would be helpful if you allowed me to take the lead. I suspected something wasn't quite right while you and your associates unwittingly contributed details."

Before she could even formulate an answer, Mark shook his head. Did he think she'd allow the security director to take credit for all their hard work? What she really objected to was the word *unwittingly*. It made it sound like she was a ditzy old lady, which she certainly was not.

The hand not balled on her hip went up. She pointed her index finger again as she spoke. "First, you should know I am a seasoned sleuth. Mark," she cut her chin in his direction, "is a thirty-plus year police officer, now detective. He has solved numerous cases with many being murders. Truthfully, I think it is unlikely that you would have solved this case on your own. This is what the police will think. Maybe you should say Detective Mark Taber consulted on the case." The point made, she returned her hand to her side.

He continued stroking his mustache, but then allowed his hand to drop. "This sounds workable, but..." He held up a finger mirroring Donna's earlier actions, "…What's in it for you?"

Since it seemed as if she gave up all claim to solving the case, she'd wait the tiniest bit, letting him think he had received everything he asked for. When Ramirez dropped eye contact and turned to Mark for an answer, she knew she had waited a tad too long.

"I'd like another cruise, free, of course."

"A free cruise!" His hands fluttered in the air as if he were ready for take-off. "That's impossible!"

"No, it isn't." It probably wouldn't be an appropriate time to mention she'd researched the matter before stepping onto the ship. Not that she had any plans at the start to ask for reimbursement since she had planned to sun by the pool while various crew members waited on her. What she wanted to be sure of, before booking her cruise, was that she had chosen the line with the least number of lawsuits filed against it, which she did. "I've read about cruise lines offering credit for a new cruise when something horribly goes wrong."

"That applies to a fire or the entire ship getting sick, not playing at being a lady sleuth."

"You shouldn't have said that." Mark murmured under his breath, then shot the confused security director a pitying look.

"I shouldn't have said what?" The sly, slightly superior director was gone leaving a bewildered man in his place.

"*Play!* I wasn't playing when I hunted down clues. Nor was I playing when I spoke to the suspects. Should I ask what you were doing when I was supposedly…" She put her fingers up to make air quotes, "…playing."

"He pushed his shoulders back and thrust his chin out. "I was conducting the ship's business."

Donna considered mentioning the casual chit chat that the director made with the various passengers when he wasn't hanging out at the pool ogling bikini-clad women, but she didn't. Instead, she changed tactics. "You did help when Maria went into labor. Anyone dealing with Heloise when she was in full rage deserves some sympathy."

"Yes, yes. This is true. I'm sorry for saying *playing*. I misspoke. My English isn't so good."

She had her doubts about the last part since any ship that carried mostly Americans would hire a security director who could speak English fluently, but she'd give him that one. "The cruise?" She raised her eyebrows.

"I'll see what I can do. Perhaps a discount, maybe half off?"

"Let me think about it."

Mark made a face at her reply then mouthed the words, *take it. Honeymoon.*

It would be nice to get away, especially in the winter. "Don't we have some people to see?"

"Of course, right this way." He opened the door as Mark gathered his sports coat and Donna picked up her purse.

They both followed the man keeping back far enough in the hall for Mark to whisper. "You should take the half price cruise. It would make a good honeymoon. This time we can get on the ship together."

"I plan on it, but no reason to let him know just yet. Especially since I have to hold a straight face while he makes himself out to be the hero."

His fingers entangled with hers. "Don't worry. We both know the truth. That's what matters."

"I agree." She gave his hand a squeeze while Ramirez stood by the elevator clapping his hands.

"Hurry! We don't have all day."

Maybe she should hold out for seventy-five percent off. The way he immediately offered the half-off discount meant that it was the standard compensation package. You'd think for the services of two skilled professionals, they could be a touch more grateful.

The freight elevator shot downward without the three of them saying anything. Perhaps the men were thinking about their statements, but Donna had already moved on to the wedding plans. Since neither one of them was getting any younger, there was no reason to plan a blowout wedding. Once home, she'd contact Herman, who was a justice of the peace and she suspected he'd be itching for a return visit to his former home of Legacy. He might even bring some of his friends along, so she'd need to have rooms open for them, which meant the wedding couldn't be during the busy season.

Summer could be busy. As well as Fall when Columbus Days occurred. The entire town re-enacted one of Columbus's ships shipwrecking off the coast of North Carolina. Even though originally Columbus was supposed to have landed on Christmas, everyone agreed that sailing was not a winter sport in North Carolina. Last year, they couldn't even round up three tall sailing ships and had to settle for one cabin sailboat, a smaller Hobie Cat, and Jamison's Motors pontoon boat, which had a picture of a tall ship painted to one side along with the name of the company stenciled across it.

The elevator shuttered to a stop and Mark reached for her hand. Ramirez led them past the waiting people milling slightly as they shuffled their carry-ons behinds them. As they passed the group, a few grumbled about Mark and Donna getting preferential treatment.

By the time they reached a Staff Only door, comments concerning them being arrested for smuggling now floated through the corridor. One lady piped up loud enough for Donna to hear.

"She even tried to get me to buy an ivory bracelet. You know those things are taboo."

The words stopped her. *Smugglers*? Did they look like smugglers? Wait a minute, that voice sounded familiar. Heloise. She should have known. Even though she wanted to correct Heloise and explain ivory was outright banned as opposed to being tabooed, a slight jerk on her hand had her looking up at her fiancé who still had hold of her hand.

"Ignore her. Gossipers gossip. End of story."

Maybe. In the end, it made her sound rather mysterious. Not that smuggling was ever on her bucket list as something she wanted to do. Right now, getting home, seeing her dog, and everything getting back to normal sounded just about perfect. Although, normal tended to be a relative word at the Painted Lady Inn. If all went well, no one would die in her vicinity in the next six months. With her free hand, she crossed her fingers just to be sure.

<u>Discover The Painted Lady Inn Mysteries Series</u>

Murder Mansion

Drop Dead Handsome

Killer Review

Christmas Calamity

Death Pledges a Sorority

Caribbean Catastrophe

Weddings Can Be Murder

Author Notes

A Bark in The Night was written after many requests from the local readers for a story set in Indianapolis. I certainly knew the town and surrounding areas. Many of the businesses and streets mentioned in the story do exist. While the characters and the very lovable Max are entirely my creation.

Come and visit Indianapolis some time. You might be surprised at its several first-class restaurants and venues. I even have an adorable bed and breakfast to recommend too, The Nestle Inn.

Love to see you. In the meantime, stay in touch via my newsletter. Sign up at www.morgankwyatt.com.

Subscribers find out about exclusive freebies, contests, and personal appearances.

If you feel like writing a review, please do.

Reading takes you to your happy place.

MK Scott
www.morgankwyatt.com

www.ingramcontent.com/pod-product-compliance
Lightning Source LLC
Chambersburg PA
CBHW060435180626

46817CB00007B/2817